Hol

CLAIRE KENT

ONE

Find the strongest man there. Give yourself to him in return for protection. It's the only way you'll ever survive.

The words kept ringing in Riana's head. She knew they were intended as a kindness, and in her gut she knew they were true. But they made her want to scream anyway.

Genus 6 was a prison planet.

It wasn't a penal colony. The Coalition had given up on those long ago when too many exiles managed to escape and make it back to the civilized planets—sometimes even as far as Earth. So instead of colonies, the Coalition had assigned otherwise uninhabitable planets as primitive and inescapable prisons. The surface of Genus 6 was covered by a volatile ocean that was poison to human life. The prison hold was built beneath that ocean. Even if a convict managed to get through the structural barriers and the guards, there was no way to survive the ocean.

Genus 6 was hell as far as Riana was concerned.

There were any number of prison planets in the Coalition now, and Riana had never given them a second thought. She'd heard horror stories—as everyone had—about people unjustly incarcerated and permanently caged up like animals. Stories like that weren't unusual. The Coalition Council, the ruling body of civilized space, made up of representatives from all the major planets, wasn't known for using its authority in a fair or enlightened way.

But it wasn't something Riana had wasted any time or indignation on.

Life sucked sometimes. The Coalition sucked most of the time. And there wasn't anything anyone could do about it.

So she minded her own business and flew her expeditions under the Coalition radar. Archeologists weren't particularly valued at present—as they provided neither power nor money for those in authority. They were usually ignored though.

Which was the way Riana had always preferred it.

She was on staff with an Earth university but hadn't been on campus for nearly four years. She spent all her time at her digs—usually on obscure, aging planets where civilization had died out centuries ago. She'd been orphaned as a child and raised by a grandmother who'd died ten years ago. She'd never had many friends. Her professional colleagues were all she needed for companionship.

Mostly she just wanted to be left alone to do her work.

And she had been—for the eight years since she'd earned her degree. Until she'd happened to choose the wrong place to dig.

All archeological digs had to be approved by the Coalition well in advance of the project. Riana had gone through all the necessary red tape and had received permission for her work on the Imperial Palace of Karna. And if she'd assumed that permission had extended to the grounds surrounding the Palace, that had been her mistake.

A mistake for which she would pay for the rest of her life.

A life that might not last very long.

There were no light sentences in the Coalition. All official crimes were treated the same—from trespassing to murder. If a crime wasn't a threat to Coalition authority or resources, it was usually ignored. So Riana assumed there must have been some sort of covert Coalition headquarters elsewhere on Karna, or her breaking of the rules and trespassing on the grounds would never have been prosecuted.

It *was* prosecuted though, and she was summarily convicted.

Then she was sentenced to imprisonment on Genus 6, the closest prison planet to Karna.

There were no specified terms on prison sentences for the Coalition. Those who went in never came out.

One other prisoner had been transported to Genus 6 with her—a sleazy, middle-aged man with thinning hair and a nauseating leer. The transport landed on water since there was no other way of landing on Genus 6. The spacecraft must have been designed to be a submersible as well since it then submerged to the prison structure beneath the ocean.

After it had docked, she and the other prisoner were hauled into the main guardroom. The room was foul—dirty and smelling strongly of stale sweat and faintly of urine. They were shackled in mechanized manacles while the paperwork was taken care of, and Riana shuddered with disgust at the stench and at the lewd suggestions her fellow prisoner kept muttering about how he was planning to take her when they were finally dumped into the main prison hold.

She'd been in shock for the past two days—ever since she'd learned what her fate would be. The shock was a blessing since it had kept her from fully processing what was going to happen to her here.

There looked to be about a dozen guards in the room, but Riana's attention was held by the man who appeared to be in charge. He introduced himself curtly to the transport officials as Davis and gave Riana and the other prisoner a cursory inspection.

Davis must have been in his forties, with slightly graying dark hair, strong features, and sharp green eyes. He didn't have the crude quality of the other guards, but he was all business, with no softness in his expression.

He barely seemed to notice Riana, but some of the other guards did, ogling or making crass comments about her body.

She wasn't any sort of beauty queen or sex symbol. She had a pretty good body, dark curly hair, and blue-gray eyes. Nothing about her was particularly extraordinary, but she was a basically attractive female in a setting where that was clearly rare.

Riana had never felt so objectified in her life, and the terror that had been held back by the shock of incomprehension was starting to take shape in her gut.

This was real. She was really a prisoner about to be thrown into a prison hold with a couple hundred rough, violent criminals. With no mercy and no protection.

She'd be lucky if she made it through the night.

One of the guards, eyeing Riana offensively, said, "Maybe we should give her a test drive before we hand her down to the animals."

Davis stepped over and backhanded him across the jaw—the gesture more effective because of its perfect blandness. "That's the way to lose your post. We aren't responsible for what the prisoners do in the Hold, but we are responsible for what happens outside it."

The words weren't much comfort to Riana, who was about to be thrown down into the Hold.

"Don't worry," her sleazy fellow prisoner said. "I'll take care of the test drive myself."

To Riana's disappointment, Davis didn't strike the sleaze. Instead, he calmly pushed her toward what appeared to be a small armored vehicle.

It was then he leaned down to murmur in her ear the words that changed everything. "Find the strongest man there," Davis said. "Give yourself to him in return for protection. It's the only way you'll ever survive."

The advice made sense. She'd never be able to protect herself. Not in a place like this. If she didn't seek protection from someone who was strong enough to give it to her, she'd be literally ripped apart.

But the alternative was equally unappealing. Giving herself to one of the prisoners—becoming a kind of voluntary sex slave—sounded like it might be worse than death.

She didn't have time to dwell on the dilemma for very long. Once the sleaze was hauled into the vehicle as well, the door was closed and Davis sat down at the controls.

The vehicle was lowered into a cavernous room.

The Hold.

As soon as they touched down, Riana realized why the vehicle was so heavily armed. A single guard wouldn't dare to enter the Hold without some serious defense.

Prisons like this didn't have individually assigned cells, and there was no separation of genders. It was a free-for-all. Mass chaos. A nightmare of violence and primitive power. Survival was based on physical prowess and strategic alliances. The weak and those without protection starved, or they were murdered, assaulted, or raped.

That could very easily be her.

"I'll take you around the Hold so you can see the layout," Davis explained, "before I let you out."

Again, Riana realized it was an unnecessary kindness — giving the new prisoners time to scope things out before they had to handle the initial arrival.

As soon as her eyes adjusted to the dimmer light of the Hold, Riana could see that the structure had once been set up like a more traditional prison. There were rows of cells lining the walls on both sides—three levels of them. But few of them had doors or bars, so they'd neither keep one in nor keep others out.

Glancing into one of the open cells, Riana saw a naked man on his knees with another man's cock in his mouth.

She looked away immediately, feeling bile rise in her throat.

What was going to happen to her here?

"Food comes twice a day," Davis explained disinterestedly. "It's passed down through the chute there." He gestured toward the center of the back wall. "Obviously, it doesn't make it around evenly."

Riana had no doubts about that. It wouldn't be individually portioned, so the strongest would take what they wanted—leaving the rest to make do with what was left.

Davis paused in front of a large cell—twice as big as the others. Looking in, Riana realized that was because the wall between two cells had been torn down to make one big one.

"That's Thorn. He's someone to pay attention to." Davis glanced back, giving Riana a significant look.

Riana peered more closely and saw a handsome blond man stretched out on a bed. He was dressed in trousers and a T-shirt, and he appeared to be talking to someone. She noticed that there were three women in the large cell—all in various states of undress—and Riana realized why Davis had given her that look.

This must be the alpha male of the Hold. He already had three women under his protection. He would be the obvious choice for Riana too.

She couldn't see the women very well. The one closest to her was wearing a tattered, revealing dress. She had probably been attractive at one time, but she now looked dirty, prematurely old, and used up.

Riana experienced another surge of nausea and tried to fight back her rising panic.

"Toilets," Davis said, pointing to the right. A doorway—without a door—led into what must be the main bathrooms.

Riana gasped as she saw a man getting beaten by two others just in front of it.

There was no reason to be surprised though. This was what happened on a prison planet.

Davis appeared not to notice the fight and kept steering the vehicle around the perimeter of the Hold.

They were nearing the end of the opposite side when Riana noticed a particular cell set off by itself.

It was the same size as all the others, except this one had metal bars intact and a functional door. Looking through the wall of bars, she noticed a large man doing one-arm push-ups inside.

He had olive skin, and his dark hair was shaved down close to the scalp. He was really big—tall, broad shoulders, muscular arms and legs—and he was wearing a worn, sleeveless T-shirt.

Something about him fascinated Riana, and she stared as Davis explained something about a system of rewards for "good" behavior.

The man finished his push-ups and stood, coming over to the bars to stare out at the vehicle. His face wasn't classically handsome, but the broad forehead, high cheekbones, and square jaw looked both powerful and compelling.

"Who is that?" Riana asked.

Davis glanced over at the man. "He'd never give his name. He's been here for a year now. He's a loner. Keeps to himself."

Riana stared more closely and realized the man must be able to lock himself in his cell—which had to be a real privilege in a place like this. She also noticed a doorway at the back of his cell and saw the edge of what looked like a primitive toilet inside.

This man had the only cell with a private toilet in the entire Hold.

That fact told Riana something she needed to know.

"And that's it," Davis said, circling the vehicle back around to where they'd come in. "Time to disembark."

Which was a polite way of saying they were now going to be dumped into the Hold.

Her mind suddenly became a frantic blur. Riana could barely breathe, much less follow distinct movements as the back door of the vehicle opened and deposited her and the sleaze on the hard, cold floor.

The door immediately closed behind them, and then their manacles clattered to the floor as Davis released them remotely.

Riana shook off her hands, restoring circulation. She was freed of the shackles.

But now she was in more danger than ever before in her life.

The circling vehicle had gained everyone's attention, and already other prisoners—most of them hard-eyed and dirty, more like beasts than like men—were starting to approach.

She was so focused on the impending danger and her rising terror that she failed to notice the sleaze who'd been dropped off with her.

He made a quick grab for her breast—perhaps thinking he'd better grope while he could, before stronger competition approached.

Riana reacted instinctively. She gave a hard sideways kick, landing it precisely on his groin. She wasn't physically helpless. Her work required physical labor, and she had always been in good shape—her body long, slender, and fit. She also knew a few basic self-defense moves, as any independent woman did if she traveled alone on the outskirts of Coalition space.

With a strangled grunt, the sleaze doubled over. She aimed another kick, this one at his face, which was easily accessible because he was leaning over.

Her foot slammed into his mouth and jaw, knocking him backward. He gave an agonized howl.

She wished she'd knocked a few teeth out, but her kick hadn't been quite strong enough for that.

Her easy victory over her fellow prisoner caused a murmur of responses through the Hold. There was also some derisive laughter—hopefully aimed at the sleaze—and a few appreciative whistles.

She wasn't fooled. She wasn't going to get herself through this on her own. The guy she'd clobbered had been a scrawny coward. She wouldn't have a chance against at least half the men she saw circling around her.

"A cunt," a nasal voice called out. "It's about time we got a new one."

Riana willed herself not to be sick.

She remembered Davis's words.

Find the strongest man here. She needed to find the strongest man here.

The first man she saw distinctly was frightening. At least a foot taller than she was and made like a bull with an oversized chest and unpleasantly beefy arms. He had a long, dark braid down his back, and his bare chest was covered with tattoos.

He approached her, eyeing her up and down with an objectifying stare that made her feel like she was naked.

"Thorn will want her," someone said from the sidelines.

The man turned his head with a sneer as if defying anyone who would assert that Thorn had a stronger claim to her than him.

"How are you with your mouth?" he asked. He turned back to pin her down with a merciless gaze.

Riana swallowed hard. Her mouth was so dry she couldn't speak, and her heart was hammering in her chest so painfully she thought it might explode.

This man would eat her alive.

There wasn't any miraculous rescue in this place. No authority to keep any sort of order. Her only chance of survival was to be smarter than anyone else.

And to ally herself with exactly the right man.

That man—by all appearances—was approaching even now, swaggering with the kind of confident authority that showed his position in this primitive community.

Thorn's clothes were in better shape than anyone else's. He also looked well fed and rested, which wasn't the case with at least half the people she could see from where she stood. He had a kind of entourage—some men who acted like bodyguards and the women Riana had noticed before.

Riana had met his type before. Arrogant, entitled, confident of their own physical prowess. The kind of superficial alpha male you could find in every ship, bar, and gym in Coalition space.

"Were you going to make a play for her, Asp?" Thorn asked, facing the other man with a manner bristling with testosterone.

It was a silent battle—a wordless duel of power and intimidation.

Riana looked on without breathing, wondering if Asp would back down or if they'd actually get in a fight over her.

It wasn't a romantic fantasy. It was more like ghastly horror. Both of these men would just use her until she was entirely used up.

Thorn might not be as innately brutal as Asp seemed to be, but Thorn was utterly selfish—she could tell that from the first look—and he hadn't become the alpha male around here by treating other people as human beings.

Asp eventually backed down, muttering something under his breath as he slunk away in disgust.

Riana was hardly relieved. At least a fight would have delayed the inevitable.

But the inevitable was fast approaching. Thorn stepped closer to her, and his eyes crawled over her body from her shoulder-length curls to her sensible shoes.

"Are you a whore?" he asked blandly.

"No." She was so surprised by the question that she managed to speak over the rancid texture in her mouth.

"Good. I don't do whores although they're usually all we get down here. You have a good body, which is the only other thing I require in a woman. Two options." His eyes—a very dark blue—narrowed as he explained, "Be my woman. Do what I tell you. I'll keep you safe. Or if you refuse, I'll turn you over to the rest of them."

He gestured back to "the rest of them." Riana's mind was in too great a blur to see distinct faces, but the rest of the prisoners seemed to be lurking just in the background, like a hungry pack of wolves.

"They'll take turns using you until they're bored. You won't last the night."

Riana knew his final words weren't an exaggeration. It was possible some lesser alpha male might try to take her as his, but he probably wouldn't be strong enough to keep her safe from the others for long.

"What's your decision?" Thorn demanded, looking slightly annoyed at her hesitation.

This was the moment. The one that would decide her fate.

Common sense, social pressure, and nearly all the evidence told her to take Thorn up on his offer.

Let him fuck her. Let him keep her alive.

Riana glanced around the prison one more time, and her eyes landed on the barred cell of the loner whose name Davis hadn't known. In the back of her mind, she'd noticed he'd stepped over to watch when she'd laid out the sleaze a minute ago.

Now he was standing silently, one hand resting loosely on a bar.

Her eyes met his for a few seconds, and she saw something there she hadn't seen in anyone else's here.

It wasn't kindness or pity or mercy or anything soft.

She couldn't really name what she'd seen, but it reminded her of independence.

She turned back to Thorn.

He was waiting, a smirk of pleased entitlement on his handsome face, as if he never doubted what her answer would be.

That did it. She ignored her reason and followed her instinct.

She turned on her heel and kicked out again, this time landing the blow right on Thorn's hard, flat stomach.

He grunted and took a step backward, more in surprise than real pain.

It was a good kick, but there was no way she could outmaneuver him physically.

"I don't want you or them," Riana said loudly, turning her head to look back at the loner in his cell, giving him a significant gaze she could only hope he'd respond to.

A wash of rage transformed Thorn's face, intensifying when other prisoners started to snicker a little.

Thorn advanced on her like a stalking animal. "We'll go with the third alternative," he gritted out. "I'll take you first and then throw what's left back to the rest of them."

It wasn't an idle threat. Riana knew he would act on it. She would be beaten and raped and then given to others who would do it to her again and again.

She looked back at the loner and felt a wave of absolute despair when she saw he'd turned his back. On her. On the rest of the prison.

He wasn't going to respond after all.

Which meant there was absolutely no hope for her.

Riana gulped in what air she could over the strangling lump in her throat and turned to face Thorn with the last bit of courage she possessed.

She'd gambled on the wrong man it seemed. Foolishly. Impulsively. And now she was going to face the consequences.

Thorn made a grab for her hair, which was in a no-nonsense ponytail. She jerked away but not quickly enough.

He snatched a handful of hair and used it to drag her closer to him, the pull on her scalp so brutal she wanted to cry.

She didn't cry. Instead, she fought back blindly, doing all she could to knee him in the groin. She landed a glancing blow, one that made him huff, but it wasn't effective enough to cause him to loosen his hold.

Her fingernails clawed at his chest, trying to gouge him deeply enough to hurt. Her struggles were futile though, as she'd known they'd be.

He twisted her around until her back was against his chest and one powerful arm imprisoned her around the waist.

Then something happened. She was suddenly freed, stumbling away with a whimper of shock, pain, and relief.

She turned around to see the loner standing in front of a gasping Thorn, whom he must have just punched on the side.

"What the fuck," Thorn rasped, staring in astonishment up at the other man. "Do you actually want to claim the little bitch?"

The loner didn't say anything. His expression was stoic, unmoving, and his eyes never left Thorn's.

When Thorn swung at him, the man caught the fist and began to twist Thorn's arm around his back. Thorn wasn't a weakling, so the physical power in the move was as shocking as it was impressive.

Thorn managed to pull away and got a swing in at the other man's abdomen. It landed but didn't have any evident effect. The other man kept coming, lashing out at Thorn with both his arm and his leg, leaving Thorn doubled over and winded.

No one interfered. It must be some kind of archaic code of honor among criminals.

The whole Hold was buzzing with astonished reaction to the scene, but Riana couldn't look away from the two men fighting.

She was still terrified but for a different reason now. She knew which man was going to win this fight.

She was just scared of what would happen afterward when she had to give herself to him.

The loner swung again and this time missed as Thorn finally managed to get in a good move. He leveled a blow at the other man's face, and his fist glanced off the side of his jaw, leaving blood in its wake.

After that it was a desperate, primitive wrestling match in which it was impossible to pinpoint distinct moves. The two men were well matched, grappling in a tangle of limbs for several minutes before the loner leveled the final blow.

Thorn lay on the floor, bloody and gasping. The loner stood up—not in great shape himself—but he was as stoic and silent as ever as he walked over to Riana.

Their eyes met, and she noticed that his were a startling shade of blue in his dark face. She swallowed and tried to say something but couldn't think of anything to say.

The other criminals stepped aside, clearly intimidated by the man who'd just defeated their alpha.

It had been a risk, but Riana had thought he might. He didn't have the biggest cell, but he had the best one—with bars and the private toilet. He would have had to successfully defeat others to win it. Just because he didn't mingle in the warped community that constituted the prison didn't mean he wasn't more than capable of tackling it.

She had no hopes that he'd be kind, gentle, or loving. But looking at him didn't sicken her like looking at everyone else she'd seen here.

If she was going to fuck anyone, it was going to be him.

He didn't say a word as he faced her, and after a minute he took the back of her shirt in his hand and used his grip on it to push her forward toward his cell. He'd understood the silent agreement as much as she had.

She walked with him willingly—although she clearly didn't have much choice in the matter. He was a little rougher than she was comfortable with when he pushed her into his cell and stepped in afterward.

He locked the barred door behind them. The click of the lock was both horrifying and a relief.

Now she was locked in this cell with a nameless criminal.

But at least all the rest of them were locked out.

The cell wasn't very large. There was room enough for a bed with a thin mattress attached to the wall, a metal table with one drawer—also attached to the wall—and a bulky object covered by a tattered sheet in one corner. There was also an ancient, battered sink in the opposite corner that appeared to have working water—another rare luxury in this hellhole.

Riana stood in the middle of the floor and waited, something inside her shuddering.

The man gestured into the small nook with the toilet. "You can use it."

His voice was curt and gruff, and his stare was utterly blank.

She limped toward the bathroom, a little sore from her scuffle with Thorn. "Thanks." She meant it. No matter how abrupt the offer, it was a generous gesture. She shivered at the thought of having to face the horror of the shared bathroom where she'd be threatened every moment.

When she got into the bathroom, she was brutally aware of the fact that there wasn't a door. So she was grateful that he didn't stand and watch her as she went—which he could have insisted on.

Instead, he stepped away, and she heard him turn on the water in the sink.

The toilet was an archaic one that ran with plumbing, but Riana was hardly going to complain as she flushed it. When she came out, she saw that the man was leaning over and splashing water on his face.

He even had a couple of towels. She wondered how he'd gotten his hands on them.

"Is your face okay?" she asked weakly as she noticed him wiping away the blood.

"Fine."

He sure wasn't much of a conversationalist.

"I'm Riana." She had no idea what she was supposed to do. Her knees were shaky, so she sank down to perch on the edge of the bed.

"Okay."

She blinked. He wasn't even going to tell her his name?

"Thanks," she began, trying to speak clearly despite her nerves. "For your help. I mean, for..."

He turned around and stared down at her.

The man was pure physicality. His closely shaved dark hair emphasized the sculpted curve of his skull. His olive skin —it must be natural since there was no sun to tan his skin here—was covered with a sheen of perspiration. He was wearing the kind of sleeveless T-shirt her grandmother had called a "wifebeater," and it showed off his impressive shoulders and the rippling muscles of his arms. His well-worn trousers were slung low on lean hips. His large build was natural too and—although he was obviously in excellent shape—he didn't look fake or overblown like Asp.

His features too starkly chiseled and his expression too impassive to be labeled traditionally handsome. But power and masculinity radiated off him in waves.

"Do you think I helped you out of the goodness of my heart?"

It was the longest sentence she'd heard him utter, and it made her heart leap into her throat. "Uh, no, but I'm still grateful."

"No gratitude. I'm getting something in return." His blue eyes seemed to impale her. "Right?"

She gulped. "Right."

Never for a minute had she hoped he would generously give her a pass. Of course she was going to have to fuck him.

He took three steps over until he was standing next to the bed, directly in front of where she was sitting. "Take off your shirt."

Riana gasped and darted her eyes over to the bars of the cell. The other prisoners were still milling outside, some blatantly staring at the two of them inside.

He followed her look. "There's no privacy here. You'll get used to it."

When he didn't say anything else, she realized she was going to have to deal with the embarrassment. With trembling fingers, she started to undo the buttons on the front of her shirt.

The man watched her. His face didn't change, but she thought she saw something almost hungry in his gaze when she dared to meet his eyes.

When she'd unbuttoned her shirt, she slowly pushed it off over her shoulders, left only in her stretchy camisole.

"That one too," the man directed, his voice even lower and thicker than before.

Might as well get it over with. Riana turned on the bed so she wouldn't expose her breasts to any passing ogler and pulled her camisole off over her head.

Her bare breasts jiggled slightly from the motion. She didn't have an extraordinarily voluptuous figure. Her limbs were long and lean, and she'd always been fairly athletic. But her breasts were firm and rounded, so she hoped he wouldn't be disappointed.

She was almost as terrified of his deciding not to bother with her as she was of having him fuck her.

He didn't appear to be disappointed although it was almost impossible to read anything on his face. He leaned down, pushing her down onto her back on the bed. He reached out to cup her breasts—not caressing as much as feeling them. His gaze devoured her half-naked form.

She tried to block out the crude laughter from outside the cell. At least his body now mostly shielded her nakedness from outsiders.

His hands were big and calloused, and they felt rough against her skin. Her nipples had peaked from the cool air and his touch, but she was far too scared to feel any pleasure.

Her chest rose and fell rapidly as he slid his hands down from her breasts to her flat belly.

When his fingers hooked around the waistband of her pants, she couldn't hold back a little whimper of fear.

He paused, and his eyes returned to her face. "I don't get off on pain," he muttered.

Riana swallowed hard and realized what he was telling her. It was a comfort. More of a comfort than she'd expected.

He wasn't going to hurt her. At least not intentionally.

She could fuck him. She'd fucked men she didn't know very well before. The last man she'd slept with had been two years ago—a one-night stand with a guy she'd met in a bar. It had left her feeling kind of icky, and she'd been avoiding sexual entanglements since then. She'd never had any hopes of falling in love in a traditional romance, so it hadn't been all that hard to go without.

She had sexual urges like everyone else, but there were simpler ways of dealing with those.

It had been a while for her, but she could fuck this man. He was a better choice than anyone else here. He wasn't ugly or nauseating, and he didn't appear to be out to hurt or humiliate her.

She took a few, slow deep breaths and nodded at him.

He must have taken that as her sign of acceptance because he returned to unfastening her pants.

She lifted up her hips so he could pull them off with her panties.

The man stared down at her groin, that hungry look appearing again in his eyes.

Riana panted in nervous gasps, trying to will her body to relax.

He reached down and parted her intimate folds, pressing his thumb against her clit.

She made a little mew in response, feeling a surreal kind of disbelief that this was actually happening to her.

Using his thumb to rub her clit in little circles, the man kept devouring her body with his gaze.

Then she realized what he was doing. Trying to turn her on so she'd be wet enough for him to enter comfortably.

"Rub your breasts," he said, sustaining the massage with this thumb.

She obeyed his direction, flushing in embarrassment but realizing it was a good idea. The wetter she was, the better it would be. It was actually a generous gesture on his part.

He could have just thrust into her dry and started pounding away.

A lot of men would.

She twirled her nipples between her fingers and thumbs and felt the tugs at her pussy in response. She forced her breathing to slow, taking deep inhalations and long exhalations.

His thumb on her clit helped, and her body finally began to relax. She felt the beginnings of pressure between her legs although her heart was still pounding brutally in her chest.

The man readjusted his hand, sliding his finger into her pussy to test her readiness. She was a little bit wet now, and the feel of his finger inside her, combined with his thumb on her clit and her own fondling of her breasts, caused a sudden jolt of pleasure to surprise her.

She gasped and arched up slightly, her mouth falling open on the taken breath.

He grunted and pulled his hand from between her legs. "Fuck." Something hot had flared up in his gaze, and he began to fumble at the fastenings of his pants.

Riana stared, realizing with a clench in her belly that he wasn't able to wait any longer.

He freed his cock although Riana didn't look down at it—afraid the sight of such an intimate part of his body would push her anxiety over the edge. Then he positioned himself between her legs and lined up his erection at her entrance.

She still wasn't very wet, so he used his saliva to slick his cock up before he pushed it into her pussy.

He was big, and she was tight. And even with his attempts to make it easier, the stretching of her inner walls was intense and uncomfortable.

Riana whimpered, her hands flying up to clutch at the pillow beneath her head.

"Fuck, you're tight." His face twisted, and his head jerked to the side, his breath hitching in his throat. "Okay?"

She couldn't say no. This was his payment for protecting her and letting her survive. She took two long deep breaths, willing her inner muscles to relax against the penetration. "Yeah."

His eased his hips back and then forward again in a small, experimental thrust. His cock moved pretty easily inside her, and the discomfort was easing up some.

He'd reared up on straightened arms, holding his chest off hers. Since she had room, Riana squeezed her hand down between their pelvises so she could rub at her clit.

The stimulation had the immediate effect of distracting her from the tight stretching. So when he began to thrust for real, it was neither painful nor unpleasant.

He was panting above her now and sweating, and he made soft grunts every time he pitched his hips forward.

Riana bent her knees up higher and rubbed her clit hard and fast. It wasn't bad. She could do this. He was an attractive, masculine man, and he was taking it pretty easy on her. Maybe eventually she could even enjoy it.

Then she happened to glance over his powerfully built shoulder and noticed a few prisoners standing in front of the cell, staring blatantly as he fucked her.

She whimpered again, her body washed in the heat of mortification as she imagined what they were seeing.

The man paused with a thick hitch of his breath at the pitiful sound she made. He must have recognized what she had noticed.

With a guttural sound, he jerked his head back to glare at the onlookers. "Back off," he bit out, the words almost a snarl.

They backed off.

Riana felt the oddest sensation in her chest. A weird, unnerving kind of satisfaction. That everyone else feared him and that he was fucking her.

"Thanks," she whispered, stretching beneath him and trying to loosen her muscles even more.

He didn't respond except with a curt nod. Then he began to thrust again.

This time when she started up her massage of her clit, she felt her pussy clench in response. Suddenly realizing that she should probably try to be a better fuck, lest he decide she wasn't enjoyable enough for him to bother with, she tried to pump her hips a little, matching the rhythm of his steady thrusts.

She gasped and arched up as she felt another tug of pleasure shoot down to her pussy.

"Fuck!" he gritted out, his face twisting again as he paused with his cock buried inside her.

Riana was panting now, and her lips parted as she stared up him. "Wha—" she began. It looked like he was in horrible pain.

He thrust again, then fell out of rhythm completely. His grunts turned rough and primal as his hips jerked and pistoned against her. "Fuck. Oh fuck!"

She parted her thighs even farther as he drove into her in hard, choppy strokes. His motion was urgent, clumsy, and animalistic, and his features contorted with pleasure and effort.

He came hard. At least it appeared he did as he let out an agonized groan and pushed into her a few last times.

He released inside her and then lowered himself over her, bending his arms for more support.

They were both gasping desperately as his body began to relax above her, the clenched muscles loosening and his stoic features softening in carnal satisfaction.

His breath was hot and damp against the skin of her cheek as he muttered, "It's been a long time for me."

He'd been here a year and apparently had fucked no one in all that time. It wasn't as long as it had been for Riana, but a year was still a significant length of time.

She wondered why he'd told her that.

She was just recognizing the gush of his semen in her pussy and assuring herself that she was up-to-date on her yearly birth control and disease treatments when suddenly all light left the cell, the entire Hold falling into pitch-darkness.

Stiffening in fear, Riana let out a strangled cry—feeling like her worst nightmares were coming true.

She didn't like total darkness, and there wasn't even the faintest trace of light left.

"Lights out," the man explained. "Same time every night."

She hadn't even realized it was night. She hadn't begun to develop a sense of timing on this planet. "I don't suppose you have a night-light?" She pitched her voice to sound unconcerned, but it was a serious question.

"There is no light at night." He slid his softening cock out of her pussy and rolled over, stretching out with what sounded like a sated groan.

Riana couldn't even see the form of his body beside her. She couldn't see anything at all. She groped around and was relieved when she felt her panties and pants on the floor. She fumbled until she'd put them on. Then she felt around on the mattress until she'd found her camisole.

The man was breathing deeply. He might have even been asleep.

Riana had no idea what she was supposed to do. The bed was small, and a bed in a place like this would be a commodity. Would he even want to share it with her at night?

There would be nowhere else for her to sleep except the floor, and she wasn't about to leave the safety of those bars and that lock.

She sat on the edge of the bed, blinking in the hopes that her eyes would adjust.

They didn't. There wasn't even light enough for her vision to adjust to the darkness. She still couldn't see anything at all.

She could sleep on the floor. Maybe he'd give her a blanket—the bed had more than one although they were all threadbare and tattered. But who knew what kind of creepy-crawlers lurked on the floor in the dark? Rats had spread from Earth to every planet in the Coalition, and every planet had its variety of bugs.

But she wasn't about to get on this man's nerves. He was by far her best choice in this hellhole.

So she got up onto shaky legs and felt blindly in front of her, trying to decide where the best place to lie down was.

"What are you doing?" The gruff words came out of the darkness, making her gasp in surprise.

She turned back toward the bed although she still couldn't see a thing. "I didn't... I didn't know if you wanted me to sleep on the bed."

There was a pause. Then, "You don't want to sleep on the floor. Trust me. You can sleep on the bed."

With a sound of relief, she groped back toward the bed, banging her shin on the frame. "Shit."

She fumbled forward, climbing in again and accidentally landing her hand on a hard, warm part of his body. "Sorry." She jerked her hand away, flushing with embarrassment. She had no idea what she'd touched. His whole body was hard and warm.

Then she felt those big, calloused hands on her thigh. They traveled up until he'd taken her by the shoulders and moved her to the opposite side of the bed. "Sleep next to the wall. I don't like feeling boxed in."

Riana had no complaints, and with a little maneuvering she stretched out next to the wall. He shared the covers with her so she felt basically comfortable—except she was hungry and a little sore between her legs.

She was finally able to relax as she pulled the covers up to her chin. The warm presence of his body beside her was oddly reassuring. Anyone would have to come through him to get to her.

It was ironic that he said he didn't like to be boxed in.

He was boxed in here. In the cell. In the Hold. On this hellish, inescapable planet.

She wondered what he'd done to get here.

Then decided she was better off not knowing.

~

She was surprised she actually fell asleep. And even more surprised that she had a sex dream, given the incongruous circumstances.

It was a dream without specific context—just brief glimpses of erotic images and tangled bodies mingled with the presence of physical desire.

When she awoke, it was still pitch-black, and Riana was hot and aroused, her face pressed up against a hard chest and her fingers groping at the belly.

Her first instinct was to sustain the activity and combine it with a humping motion against the strong leg she felt.

But then she came to her senses. Remembered where she was. And who she was with.

She jerked up with a sharp gasp. "Oh."

There was a rustling of the bedding as the man moved beneath her.

Then he grabbed her and rolled her over. She couldn't see him, but she felt him above her—his legs between hers, his hands planted on either side of her shoulders.

Her body was still pulsing with arousal and—despite the situation—she couldn't help but thrust her hips up and rub her groin against his.

If he'd been holding himself back, that move snapped the last thread of his control. He hooked his hands around her thighs and spread them so that he could rub his hard cock against the fabric of her pants, just over her pussy.

Riana whimpered and groped above her until she could claw at his shoulders.

They fumbled around until her pants were off again and her camisole was pushed up above her breasts. He lowered his mouth to one of her nipples—sucking and nipping at it until she was squirming and biting her lip to suppress her cries in response.

He didn't waste much time on foreplay. Riana's pussy was wet and aching, and she mewed in relief when he lined his cock up at her entrance and sank in.

It was tight but not uncomfortable this time. And his first thrust caused her to arch her spine and make a silly, childish sound of pleasure.

She couldn't see him at all. Just feel him—hot, urgent, and so incredibly strong—as he worked up a fast, steady rhythm of thrusts and grunts.

He kept his arms bent this time so his face was close to her—so close she could feel the panting of his breath against her hot skin. Her breasts rubbed against his chest as they rutted, and a deep pressure at her center swelled up into the beginnings of an orgasm.

Her body was moving of its own accord, pumping and rocking beneath him. Their pelvises were too close for her to squeeze her hand between, but by angling her hips she could get some stimulation of her clit from his pubic bone.

Huffing out soft, little sounds of effort, Riana clawed at his neck and shoulders. His speed accelerated, his thrusts becoming fast and clumsy, shaking the bed and her body until her breasts jiggled.

"Oh God," she gasped. "Gonna come!"

His grunts turned animalistic as he levered up on each instroke.

She came with a muffled cry, her body shaking and spasming as the pleasure pulsed through her.

He was right behind her, pushing against her contractions with a few last, rough exclamations.

His weight lowered over her as both of them started to come down. He was heavy and hot, but it wasn't unpleasant. The texture of his breath was thick and damp next to her ear.

After a minute, he pulled up and rolled over, groaning as he sprawled out on his back.

It was still too dark to see anything.

Riana was burning with lingering pleasure and with absolute embarrassment. She never would have believed she could come—have an actual orgasm, a good one—in a situation like this.

She didn't know this man. She never would have slept with him if she'd been in any normal situation.

But their blind, groping, half-asleep coupling might have been the best fuck of her life.

She'd thought he'd gone to sleep again, but suddenly his low voice wafted over toward her. "I'm Cain."

"What?"

"My name. Cain."

"Oh." She swallowed and stared up at the blackness above her. "Hi."

They lay in silence for a long time. She thought once more he'd fallen asleep, but then he surprised her by a question. "Why me?"

It seemed to come out of the blue, but she knew exactly what he was asking.

There were any number of answers to that question. There was no one better. He was the only one she could tolerate. She'd noticed the signs that revealed he could take what he wanted, even in a place like this.

But there was only one answer that mattered, so she told him the truth in the dark. "You're the strongest one here."

TWO

Riana woke up when all the lights in the Hold went on.

Blinking, she tried to adjust to the sudden brightness, feeling a pang of soreness between her legs and stickiness from not washing up after he'd ejaculated inside her twice.

She felt achy and exhausted, and her stomach felt like a heavy stone in her gut.

But at least she was alive. And healthy.

When all the odds had been against her.

Cain was still in bed too, but his eyes were open, staring fixedly at the ceiling. His arms were crossed behind his head, and the covers were pushed down around his belly.

She couldn't believe she'd fucked him. Twice. And come the second time.

She started to say something—just some trivial comment in order to break the silence—but then she stopped herself. He didn't appear to be in a conversational mood, and the last thing she wanted to do was annoy him.

After a few minutes, he glanced over at her and held her eyes with his.

He still didn't speak, however, and Riana was getting anxious about the prolonged silence.

Was he planning to tell her he'd had his fill of her already?

She wasn't the best fuck in the world, but once she warmed up she'd be better. He could at least give her more of a chance.

She actually gasped when he finally moved, so primed was she to handle whatever crisis reared its head next, but he just strode back to the bathroom.

When she heard a sudden roar of noise from outside the cell, she sat up straight in bed, her heart pounding in terror. It sounded like a riot had just exploded out of nowhere. She'd heard disturbing sounds all night—crude voices, grunts, and screams triggered by God knew what—but it hadn't been anything like this.

Cain came out of the bathroom and noticed her frozen demeanor.

"Mealtime," he explained brusquely. "It's not pretty." After quickly washing his face and hands in the sink, he shook himself off like a dog and continued, "I'll be back. You'll want to stay here."

Riana hadn't eaten in twenty-four hours, and she would soon be faint from hunger. But the sound of the madness triggered by the arrival of food—like wild cats fighting over a carcass—kept her from complaining about his plan. "Can… can you lock me in?"

"Of course. What else?"

She flushed at his impatient response and said no more as he picked up a large bowl, a bottle, and a spoon from the table, unlocked the barred door, stepped out, and locked it again behind him. There must be only one key, which he kept on him at all times.

She used the bathroom while he was gone and was relieved that there were no lurkers, slinking outside the bars to ogle or intimidate her. Mealtime must take everyone's attention.

Cain returned in less than ten minutes. He had the large bowl filled with something that smelled like stew, a hunk of bread, and two bottles. He must have found another one.

He tossed her one of the bottles, which she accepted appreciatively, gulping down the water inside.

But it would have been nice if he'd brought her some food too.

She wouldn't dream of complaining for fear of annoying him even more, but he was going to have to feed her eventually if he wanted to keep her alive to fuck her.

He put down the bowl and the bread on the table and then set down something he'd had tucked under his arm.

It was another bowl. A smaller one and empty.

Riana just stared as he spooned some of the stew from the large one into the empty one.

"How much do you want?"

Almost speechless with surprise and relief, Riana choked, "That's enough. Thanks."

He handed her the stew and broke off half the bread for her. He also had an extra spoon. She assumed he must have claimed them from one of the other prisoners.

She ate ravenously. It wasn't very good—the stew was thick and bland, and the bread was dry—but she was too hungry to care.

When she'd scraped the bottom of the bowl, Cain had already finished. He raised one eyebrow at her quizzically. "You want more?"

The riotous sounds from outside were subsiding. "It sounds like the food is gone."

"I can get more."

There was something dangerous, almost predatory about the way he said the words. Riana gulped. "I'm good. Thanks."

Not wanting to be useless, she got up from the bed and went to wash out the bowls and spoons.

Cain didn't say anything else. Instead, he did a few stretches and then started doing chin-ups on one of the horizontal bars of the cell.

She watched as he did a lengthy exercise routine—chin-ups, sit-ups, push-ups, and several other strengthening routines.

His body was gorgeous. Honed tight and powerful like a racehorse but still graceful—without the unattractively overdeveloped muscles she'd seen on several men in the prison.

He was tight and efficient and more dangerous because of it.

She pulled on her shirt over her camisole and straightened the bed but then was at a loss for what to do.

Cain wasn't any help in that department. When he'd finished his workout, he unlocked the door. "I'll be back."

Then he locked the door behind her.

She saw him take off at a run and figured maybe he ran around the Hold every morning for exercise.

And for something to do.

That was nice for him. To be able to do something.

She couldn't do anything.

Finally she moved to the far corner of the cell and ran in place for a while. Then she did some jumping jacks and then some yoga stretches.

As she was leaning over, stretching down with her hands on the floor, she became conscious of voices behind her.

She'd started to block out the constant sound of the Hold, having it blur into a vague mumble, but these voices were close.

And she could hear the words.

"Look at that ass. Makes me want to ram my dick into it until she screams."

"I'd make her scream all right."

Riana jerked up and whirled around, saw Asp standing with another prisoner. They were right at the bars, leering in at her.

And their offensive, objectifying expressions made her feel suddenly sick.

She wasn't going to show them they'd gotten to her though. With a cold glare, she bit out, "Get the fuck away."

Asp cackled maliciously. "The bitch wants to put up a fight."

"You'd think a whore would know her place."

"She knows her place. On her back with her legs spread."

Riana's vision blurred. She hadn't spent her life being coddled, and she knew how to handle herself in most situations. She'd spent her teenage years basically independent since her grandmother wasn't much of an authority, so she figured she was tougher than a lot of women.

But she'd never been confronted with that kind of coarse, demeaning objectification. Her cheeks burned with anger and mortification, and she turned her back to them.

That was a mistake.

The second man bombarded her with ribald laughter. "Looks like she prefers it from behind. Gotta love that ass."

Riana knew she shouldn't back down, but she couldn't take much more of this. Talking back to them would just encourage their verbal assault, but she was trapped in this cell, unable to get away from them.

She withstood their continued nastiness as long as she could, but it grew progressively worse.

When they started to describe what they would do when Cain got tired of the cunt and handed her to them, Riana went into the bathroom nook.

It wasn't a particularly pleasant place to hang out, but there was a wall she could hide behind.

She felt like a weakling and a coward, but at least she could put her hands over her ears and not look at them anymore.

She stayed like that for several minutes, shaking and willing herself not to be sick.

When she lowered her hands from her ears, she was relieved that their voices were no longer assaulting her.

She didn't want to go back out to the cell by herself though, like a caged animal for their disgusting entertainment.

Where the hell was Cain anyway? Selfish bastard. Taking a run and leaving her here by herself.

"Riana?"

She heard the sound of his voice before she heard the door unlocking and swinging open.

She darted back out to the cell, flushing again with mortification at the possibility of Cain catching her in her cowardice.

He was drenched in perspiration, his T-shirt sticking wetly to his chest and sweat streaming down the sides of his face. "What were you doing?"

"Nothing."

She supposed there was no chance he'd believe she was going to the bathroom. She'd been on the wrong side of the bathroom nook for that.

He stepped into the bathroom and glanced around— as if he suspected she was hiding something in there.

"What's going on?" His stoic features had tightened, and she realized it was the beginnings of anger on his face.

"I was just…" she burst out, realizing she'd better tell him the truth or he'd think something worse. "There were guys who were… I was just hiding."

To her relief, his face cleared. "I see." He turned on the water and started splashing some on his face and arms. "You need to toughen up."

"I know."

She swallowed and turned away from him, trying to fight down her automatic anger and resentment.

Who the hell did he think he was anyway? Telling her to toughen up.

She wasn't a criminal. She wasn't used to this sort of animalistic behavior.

She was a harmless archeologist who'd always minded her own business.

It wasn't her fault she got thrown into this hellhole with a bunch of beasts.

And with one arrogant, self-centered ass who treated her like an idiot.

When he finished washing up, he dried his face on a thread-thin towel. Then he peered at her, appearing to notice everything from her unnaturally stiff shoulders to her slightly protruding chin.

For the first time since she'd met him, she saw the corner of his mouth twitch up as if he were amused.

It was the only sign she'd seen that he actually possessed a sense of humor.

An infuriating sense of humor. Since it only emerged to mock her.

She bit back the sharp comment she'd been about to snap at him.

She couldn't make him mad. She was in far too precarious a situation.

Turning away from him, she stared at the floor. When she noticed he'd stopped looking at her, she did her best to pitch her voice as pleasant. "So what exactly do we do here?"

"Nothing."

"You mean there's nothing to do at all?"

Cain glanced out the bars of the cell. "You can go out and play if you want."

Riana didn't miss the snide bite in his tone, and it made her heart lurch. "I wasn't complaining," she said quickly. "I was just—"

"There's nothing to do," he said, his voice softer as if in response to her distress. "This is life here."

Nothing to do but fight for food, territory, and mates. The perfect circumstances for turning human beings into animals.

She curled up on the bed and tried not to whimper in dismay. How the hell was she going to make it through the next week? Much less the rest of her life?

Cain turned his back on her and went over to sit on the floor. He pulled the sheet off the object on the floor, and she saw that it appeared to be a pile of spare parts of metal and plastic.

She considered asking what it was but suspected he wasn't going to tell her.

So she just watched as he tinkered and eventually realized that about half the pile was put together into some sort of device.

Maybe it was a crude engine of some sort. It looked too foreign and awkward for her to tell.

She watched for an hour while he managed to fit into the mass a piece of wire he pulled out of his pocket. He must have found the wire on his run. Who knew where he located all the spare parts?

Eventually she got so bored with watching him putter around that she actually fell asleep.

She dreamed he'd created a little submersible out of the engine and used it for the two of them to escape from the prison. Then the submersible transformed into a spacecraft and rocketed them off the planet.

They had landed on some kind of paradise planet— made up of sunshine, beaches, and tropical plants—when she was awakened by a clattering sound.

She jerked into consciousness and saw immediately that he had dropped the makeshift screwdriver he was using.

He glanced over at her as he hauled himself to his feet and stretched like a big cat. "Do you want to take a walk?"

She blinked at his gruff voice, trying to process the question. "What?"

"I was going out." He nodded toward the bars of the cell to specify what he meant. "Do you want to come too, or would you rather stay here? I thought you might be getting cabin fever."

That was certainly true, but she was still nervous about making herself a nuisance. "I am. As long as you think it would be okay."

His spine stiffened almost imperceptibly. "Assuming you think I can manage to keep you safe for a few minutes."

Straightening up and rubbing her face, she said, "Of course you'll keep me safe." She was baffled that he thought she would have doubted it. "I meant, would I be too much trouble. If I can't keep up with your marathon run or whatever."

His expression cleared, and his shoulders relaxed. "I only run in the mornings. This afternoon, I'm on the hunt."

His tone wasn't particularly threatening, but Riana's mouth fell open in surprise. On the hunt? For what? It was like he'd transformed into a powerful animal, and she could suddenly see him ripping apart limbs and devouring his prey.

Like a lion. Except that wasn't right. Lions were too brightly colored and laid-back, lolling around on the grass most of the time. A bear was closer to capturing the right mood, but Cain wasn't lumbering enough for a bear.

He was sleek and dark and dangerous. Like a wolf with those blue eyes.

But wolves were pack animals, and Cain didn't run in a pack.

He was a lone hunter. Like a leopard. Agile and graceful and deadly, with hidden power in his limbs.

Cain cleared his throat and gave her a puzzled look.

Riana's cheeks flushed as she realized she'd been staring at him with her mouth open—for who knew how long—trying to find the right animal to compare him to.

"Hunting what?" she gasped. Then flushed more hotly as she heard the awed, tremulous sound of her own voice.

His thin lips twitched again—that faint sign of his sense of humor, once more directed at her. "Nothing bloody," he said as if he'd just read her mind.

He directed a pointed look over at his pile of spare parts, and she realized he must be looking for something for his device.

"Oh." She pulled herself up and straightened her shirt and her hair. Her hair was getting tangled, and she realized it would only get worse as the days passed. "I'll come with you. Thanks."

At first it was nice to get out of the cell and stretch her legs a little. Now that she knew what to expect, the Hold didn't feel so monstrous and cavernous. And while she still felt small and vulnerable, she didn't feel threatened on all sides because Cain was beside her.

She wasn't blind to the way the weaker prisoners— many toothless and nearly naked—slunk out of the way as he approached. Nor did she miss the way the stronger men bristled and gave him covert glares but didn't dare to confront him directly.

Cain wasn't an alpha male like Thorn was, demanding blatant submission, claiming power for the sake of power, and cultivating an entourage of lackeys and wannabes.

But that didn't mean people didn't recognize the threat he posed.

Especially after beating Thorn up the day before.

Riana stayed as close to Cain's side as she could, at one point shrinking into him when a gross man with a scabby face made a flailing grope for her.

Cain swatted the man away—in a move that was more efficient than angry—but it sent the man reeling back to slump against a wall.

No one approached them after that. No one tried to speak to them. Riana would have preferred it if they'd been ignored, but that was obviously not what was happening here.

Everyone was aware of them, and Riana felt painfully on display.

Cain didn't say anything to her at all. He hadn't lied when he'd said he was going on the hunt. His eyes were never still, constantly searching the cells, the prisoners, every object in the Hold as they made two laps around the perimeter.

The only distraction from the search was when the armored vehicle came up behind them. It would have run her over had Cain not pulled her out of the way.

He sneered faintly at the vehicle plowing down toward the cells at the far end.

"A new prisoner?" she asked, feeling kind of sick as she remembered the day before. She'd been sure she would be raped, tortured, killed.

It was a miracle she hadn't been.

"No. Checkup."

He spoke as if she should know what that meant, and Riana felt a flicker of annoyance when she had to press him to explain. "You want to fill me in on that?"

"Part of the Coalition's public claims about prison planets is that the prisoners' health is regularly assessed."

Riana studied him closely, a little surprised by both the articulate wording of his response and the dry intelligence of his tone. He'd seemed so purely physical—like a forceful, grunting, primal force—that she hadn't expected such a tone from him.

His eyes shifted away at her stare, but she couldn't tell if it was from boredom or discomfort.

"That's a joke," she said, responding to what he'd said. "Humans are treated worse than animals in this hole. I'm surprised they don't just kill prisoners instead of keeping us all cooped up in here. It would be cheaper that way and who would know?"

"Too many activist groups. Someone would find out."

She figured he was probably right. The Coalition Council held on to its power with a delicate balance that could be upset by any political mistake. The cost of keeping up the prisons was nothing compared to the possible political backlash. "They claim to assess our health regularly?"

"They do. And they justify it by bringing each prisoner up for 'checkup' once a year."

When he didn't say anything else, Riana just watched as what appeared to be a mechanized claw extended from the armored vehicle and clamped down around a bearded, dirty man who'd been slouching against a wall. Once it had hold of the man, the vehicle retreated back out of the Hold.

"Do I want to know?" she asked, a wave of horror passing over her as she imagined possibilities for the checkup.

"No."

That was enough for Riana. She didn't pursue the topic and tried not to think about it any further.

Instead, she watched as Cain continued his hunt, his powerful body moving in a graceful stalk as he paced around the perimeter again. She did her best to keep up.

Riana was starting to get tired, and her breath was coming out in little pants as she tried to match his stride without complaining. Finally she said, "Did you find what you needed?"

"Yes." Cain didn't say any more than that, but he directed their course toward the open space in the middle of the Hold—where there were battered tables and chairs, a few dilapidated pieces of workout equipment, and a trash chute.

Riana had noticed that a lot of the prisoners tended to mingle in that area—doing whatever it was they did to kill the time.

She reddened and sucked in a breath when she saw a grizzled man with a patch on one eye fucking a woman who was on her hands and knees. The woman must have been sixty and was the most unattractive woman Riana had ever seen. A few prisoners were looking on at the rutting with slightly bored amusement.

What kind of life must that woman lead? The idea sickened Riana even as she tried to forget the image.

Cain didn't even glance over at it, and she wondered if he had always been this callous or if living in this place had made him that way.

He headed over to a small gathering of men who seemed to be making bets on if and how fast a rat would make it up out of the trash chute.

She thought for a moment Cain was going to talk to them, but he didn't. He passed by, knocking one of them with his shoulder.

It couldn't have been accidental. Riana saw him aim with his shoulder. The man he'd knocked stumbled forward toward the trash chute. He barely caught himself in time before his foot got caught in the chute. But his stumble had startled the rat, which made a quick retreat and disappeared.

One of his companions didn't appreciate this abrupt end to their wager. He lashed out at the man who'd stumbled, smashing a fist into his jaw.

The victim fought back, and the scuffle attracted the attention of several nearby men—many of whom had been ogling Riana.

She just gaped as the fight broke out. And gaped as Cain casually turned her around, urging her back toward the cell with his hand on the small of her back.

As he passed the gaggle of onlookers, he casually bent down and picked up something from the floor, discreetly depositing it into his pocket.

Riana didn't speak until they'd returned to the cell and he'd shut and locked the door behind them.

Then she gasped, "What did you get?"

He pulled a mangled fork out of his pocket and tossed it over near his pile of salvaged treasures.

"A fork?"

He gave her a narrow-eyed look as if challenging her to cast aspersions on the worth of his find.

"Why didn't you just take it from the guy?"

He turned his back on her and faced the sink, turning on the water. "Why fight if you don't have to?"

It was a good question. It just wasn't the kind of question she would have expected a macho, dominant guy like Cain to ask himself.

He'd leaned forward to cup his hands under the running water when he sucked in a sharp breath and stiffened suddenly.

Something about the way he moved told Riana something she should have known before. "Are you hurt?"

He didn't answer. Didn't even acknowledge the question as he leaned down toward the water again.

Instinctively, Riana got up and walked over to him. "Seriously, are you hurt? I should have asked before. Was it from the fight yesterday?"

"I'm not hurt," he gritted out, reaching for a towel.

While he was distracted by drying his face, Riana pulled up the side of his T-shirt to expose the side he'd seem to favor a moment before.

His entire side was a mass of ugly, purple bruises.

"My God. Cain. My God!"

He jerked away. "They're bruises. Nothing to whine about."

"They look horrible," she said, trying to get his T-shirt pushed up more so she could see the extent of the damage. "Why didn't you say anything? And you did all those exercises this morning. It must have hurt like hell."

He gave her an unpleasant look. "Are you through?"

"No," she said, too upset to even consider whether she was being wise to press her attention on him in this matter. "Can I see how bad it is?"

"Why?"

"I know some first aid. If you broke a rib or something—"

"I didn't break a rib."

But he didn't object when she'd pushed his T-shirt up and then carefully pulled it off over his head. The bruising went from his left shoulder blade all the way down his side and forward toward his lower belly.

Riana brushed her fingers along the damage, wishing she could remember more of her medical training. "This must be why you didn't want to fight just now."

He tensed palpably. "I could have taken them easily."

"I'm sure you could," she assured him quickly. "I didn't mean to imply you couldn't." She winced as she noticed a particularly dark bruise on his lower side. "But this looks terrible. Thorn did a number on you."

Her voice had been gentle, but it was clearly the wrong thing to say—yet again. Cain stiffened and pulled away. "I promise he looks worse."

She blinked up at his closed-off face, and she realized he was still bristling with a wounded masculine ego.

What the fuck was wrong with men anyway? No matter how tough and rugged they were, they still managed to be sensitive about the slightest hint they weren't invulnerable.

"I'm sure he does," she said lightly instead of following her urge to complain about his acting like a baby. "He must look so bad he's been afraid to show his face all day."

This apparently was the right thing to say. Cain relaxed and gave a snort of what almost sounded like amusement. "I'm pretty sure I broke his nose."

"Good." She smiled and continued inspecting the damage on his body, making instinctive note of the rippling muscles of his back and the scattering of course dark hair on his chest. "I hope it heals crooked."

He didn't respond, but she saw the corner of his lips quirk up. This time it was longer than a moment. It wasn't a full-fledged smile, but it was closer than anything she'd seen.

She ran her fingers down his back—pretending to check for damage but mostly because she found the smooth, strong planes irresistible. "I wish you'd told me about your bruises before," she murmured. "Last night I mean. When we were… I hope I didn't hurt you."

He turned on his heel, so sharply she didn't expect it. Facing her, he reached out to grab her by the hips. "Nothing about last night hurt," he said, his voice as thick and rough as gravel. "I'm not that injured."

Then, as if to prove his point, he slid his big hands back until they were spanning the curve of her ass. He lifted her up to a position where she automatically wrapped her legs around his waist.

"Your bruises," she gasped, squirming as she tried not to put any pressure on his damaged side.

He started to walk, his grip so strong there was no sense in fighting it. "I told you. I'm not that injured."

He carried her over to the bed, his size and strength making her feel unexpectedly small and feminine. When he reached the bed, he lowered her onto the thin mattress and moved over her, the muscles of his arms bulging as he supported himself above her.

His eyes were so intense they seemed to devour her, and Riana felt naked despite her grungy shirt. She also felt a thrill of excitement. Anticipation.

Despite the bleakness of her situation—or perhaps because of it—her body responded to the sight of him above her. He was an attractive, virile man. Different from any man she'd ever known. She was going to have to fuck him if she wanted to stay alive.

She might as well enjoy it.

He leaned down, and her eyes widened as his face lowered toward hers—their gazes never breaking. For a moment, she thought he was going to kiss her.

But instead he shifted direction just slightly to run his lips in a line down her throat.

She tilted her head back, sucking in her breath as she felt his mouth on the sensitive skin at her pulse. He smelled strongly, but it wasn't unpleasant—it was almost a relief after the vague nastiness of the mingled odor of the Hold—and the scent of him surrounded her, intensifying her carnal response.

When he nipped at her neck slightly, she gasped at the resulting jolt of pleasure. Then she jerked her shoulders up so she could pull off her shirt. When she tossed it away, his mouth lowered even more until he mouthed her right breast through the fabric of her camisole.

She squirmed beneath him as tugs of arousal multiplied in her pussy. Her fingers groped at the back of his neck, then slid up to feel the delicious texture of the close-cropped hair on his scalp.

He adjusted his position until he was kneeling on the floor as his mouth lowered down to her middle. He pushed up her camisole to bare her flat belly, and she moaned when she felt him press hard kisses onto the sensitive skin there.

He must have unfastened her pants while she was distracted by his mouth on her belly because he pulled them off with a quick yank, taking her panties with them.

She gave a little squeal of surprise and excitement at the rough move and felt an ache of desire between her legs when he stood up beside the bed—big, primal, and powerful. She was wet. Really wet. And she was glad to see the bulge at his groin—proof that he was aroused as well.

"Turn over," he said in a thick voice, kneeling on the bed beside her.

She wasn't sure if his words had been a request or an order, and she didn't really care. Doggy style sounded pretty good to her.

She arranged herself on her hands and knees, pointing her head and shoulders away from him.

He covered her exposed bottom with both of his big hands and gave it a possessive squeeze. "Damn, you have a great ass," he muttered.

It was the first compliment he'd ever given her. And despite its crudeness, it gave her a ridiculous little thrill. She looked over her shoulder at him and felt another thrill at the smolder she saw in his eyes as he stared down at her half-naked body.

Then she saw him move one of his hands and felt two of his fingers in her slick pussy. The penetration made her gasp.

He pumped his fingers a few time, hitting her G-spot and rubbing her inner walls.

Riana gave a breathless grunt and started to pant at the delicious stimulation. Still looking back at him, she bumped her hips back toward him, trying to accelerate the rhythm.

"Fuck." Cain's voice was faint, and she couldn't tell if he was pleased, surprised, or baffled by her obvious eagerness. But before she could start to feel self-conscious, he added, "So hot."

That was okay then. So she kept pumping her ass against the penetration of his fingers, beginning to huff out little grunts that sounded almost childish as an orgasm developed more quickly than she could have expected.

Her breasts jiggled in her top, and it took some effort to keep looking over her shoulder at him kneeling behind her. But she couldn't seem to turn away from the expression on his face—hungry and intense, like he wanted to swallow her whole.

He stared down at her eager bouncing and skillfully moved his fingers in her wet pussy until her grunts turned to whimpers and then to wordless mews as he took her to the edge.

He was pushing hard against her G-spot as she came, her body jerking in clumsy spasms as the waves of release washed over her and her pussy clamped down hard around his fingers.

He sustained the contractions by pumping his fingers against the spasms, and her entire body flushed hotly as her urgency relaxed into satisfaction.

She was a little embarrassed as she darted one last look at his face, hoping he didn't think she was too easy or desperate for succumbing so easily to his advances.

For coming from nothing more than a few pumps of his fingers.

But he was already unfastening his trousers, and he looked just as eager as she had been as he aligned himself behind her, grabbing her bottom cheeks and pulling them apart so he could sink his cock into her.

She made a silly sound as the hard substance of his erection penetrated her, stretching and filling her deeply. She adjusted her hands, bracing herself on her arms so she could rock her bottom back against his pelvis.

He began to thrust immediately, his cock moving easily inside her slick pussy, and each thrust hit her in just the right way.

She couldn't look away from his expression—it was tense now, and ravenous, and so hot. At the twist in his features every time she tightened her pussy around him. She could tell he was enjoying how it felt to be buried inside her.

They were both breathing loudly, and the cot was starting to shake, squeaking shamelessly in response to their motion. The rest of the sound in the Hold blurred into a background murmur, fading against the stark urgency of their coupling.

Riana felt another orgasm beginning to build, and she gasped in both surprise and pleasure. Her neck was starting to ache, and she was losing her concentration, so she finally let her head fall forward again.

And realized they had an audience.

It wasn't the offensive onlookers of the night before. She didn't even recognize the two men who were staring in through the bars of the cell, openly gawking at their fucking.

She stifled a whimper, not wanting Cain to tell her to toughen up again. There was no privacy in this hellhole. She would need to get used to that.

Cain hadn't even seemed to notice them—the others were so insignificant to him. She needed to learn to ignore them in the same way.

But she couldn't. She couldn't stop thinking about what they must see. She was on her hands and knees on the bed, naked except for her disarranged camisole. Her tangled hair was falling into her flushed face. Her breasts and the flesh of her ass were jiggling as she pumped her hips back toward Cain's pelvis, eagerly meeting each of his thrusts. Their skin was slapping together, and Cain gripped possessive handfuls of her bottom.

And she was going to come again.

These strangers on the other side of the bars were going to see her. Coming hard from being fucked like this by a man she barely knew.

The pressure at her center tightened like a fist, sending shockwaves of pleasure into her building orgasm. "Oh God," she gasped, her vision blurring over as she bumped her bottom back against his hard strokes as rapidly as she could.

He let go of her ass and reached forward, pushing gently on her upper back until she folded her arms and lowered her shoulders to the mattress, leaving just her bottom in the air. He didn't pull back. Instead, he planted one of his hands next to her shoulder, giving him better leverage to thrust.

He wasn't pulling out much now, but his hips were pistoning against her ass, pushing into her in fast, animalistic strokes. The only sounds he made were low grunts and fast, wet breathing.

She tried to keep her eyes on the bedding just before her eyes, but she couldn't resist turning her head to look out the bars again.

The two men were still watching. One of them had his mouth hanging open. Then she heard the other one say, "Fuck. Look at her take it."

Riana whimpered and hid her face in the mattress, burning with heat that was as much shameless desire as it was mortification.

"Ignore them." The voice was low, gruff, right in her ear. Cain.

"Mm-hmm."

"Take it?" That voice was from outside the cell. The other man. "She wants it bad."

Riana tried to smother another whimper in the bedding as her whole body began to shake with intensifying need and urgency.

She did want it. She wanted it bad. And the feel of Cain's cock driving into her deep and hard was threatening to make her scream with an inexplicable pleasure.

Part of her wished that Cain would lash out at the men—making them leave the way he'd made the men leave last night.

But she somehow knew he wouldn't do that. It would make him weak. It would give the other prisoners power over him.

Over both of them.

It was a gift that he'd done so for her last night.

So she did as he said and tried to ignore the onlookers. Instead, she fought through her physical responses to find the concentration to turn back to look at Cain again.

His expression was almost twisted with what he was feeling, and there was something mesmerizing about the primitive fire in his eyes.

She felt another clench of sharp pleasure. "Oh yeah."

"Yeah?" he gritted out, his face only inches from hers.

She wasn't sure exactly what he was asking, but she answered him anyway. Her whole body was shaking—from the force of his motion now since she couldn't do much pumping in her present position—and her vision was starting to glaze over again. "Yeah," she gasped. "Gonna come. Again. Oh God!"

His thrusting intensified even more—so hard now the bed squeaked even more loudly. His grunts grew even more animalistic, guttural sounds that turned her on more than she could begin to understand.

She huffed out choppy little sounds as the agonizing pressure in her pussy finally peaked.

She buried her face in the bedding to smother her scream of release as her pussy clenched around his cock.

She was conscious of his pelvis jerking clumsily against her bottom, and she heard a rough sound as he came as well. But she couldn't think of anything except the pulsing waves of pleasure radiating from her center to saturate her body.

They left her feeling drained, exhausted, hot, and deliciously satisfied.

And really, really embarrassed.

She could feel Cain panting above her, but she couldn't bring herself to turn her head to meet his eyes immediately.

After a minute, he asked, "Okay?"

The gruff question made her able to unbury her head and look up at him. He was pulling his cock out of her pussy with a sloppy, wet sound.

"Yeah," she said with a faint smile. It was nice of him to ask—even in such an abrupt way. "That was pretty good."

The corner of his mouth twitched up. "Yeah. Pretty good."

The irony in his voice made her snicker a little, and she felt better as she curled up on the bed, trying to hide her body as best she could from whomever happened to be outside.

Cain got up, pulling up his pants and walking back toward the bathroom. When he returned, he looked normal again. He'd even pulled his T-shirt back on.

"So what are you going to do now?" she asked, curious about what else there was to do to pass the time in his cell.

He arched one eyebrow and gestured toward the fork he'd retrieved on their outing earlier. "What do you think?"

She frowned at his curt tone but watched as he went back over to the machine he was putting together out of scavenged parts.

"Oh."

"Where do you get all that stuff anyway?" she asked after a long silence.

Still focused on his work, Cain didn't glance over as he answered. "You saw me."

"I know you get them from around the Hold. But how did they get here? Surely prisoners aren't allowed to bring wire and gears and all that with them."

He didn't respond immediately, and for a minute Riana didn't think he was going to reply at all. Then he said slowly, "To keep up the pretense of treating prisoners humanely, the Coalition distributes supplies every couple of months. That's where the towels, the bedding, and the dishes come from. Sometimes they send down other things too. It just depends what kind of surplus they have on hand."

Riana thought about that for a minute. "Distribute? Does that mean they dump the supplies in a big heap and leave everyone to fight about who gets them?"

"Yep." Cain was fiddling with a piece of metal. She couldn't begin to guess what the metal used to be. "A couple of years ago, they tried to move to individual replicators for prisoners' meals instead of the feeding-trough method they use now. But that idea didn't last long."

"Don't tell me. The replicators were taken apart and made into weapons."

Cain gave a brief nod. "Evidently, in less than a week. At least that's what I'm told. The guards made a gesture at confiscating the parts, but most of them are still around in one form or another."

Obviously, Cain had scavenged many of those parts for his ungainly device.

"How did you learn how to put things together like that?" She nodded toward his device.

He shrugged. "You pick things up. I had a piece-of-junk transport that always needed fixing."

She thought about that. People didn't own transports—even junky ones—unless they traveled a lot from planet to planet. Maybe he'd been a smuggler, and that was how he'd ended up in prison.

She watched him for several minutes while she tried to enjoy the physical satisfaction of the aftermath of her orgasms and tried to ignore the crude comments that occasionally drifted her way from outside the cell.

When it was clear Cain had nothing more to say, she sniffed and stretched out on the bed. "I guess I'll take another nap."

THREE

It was still dark in the Hold. Lights out. Pitch-black. It never got any lighter than this during the imposed nighttime hours.

She couldn't see Cain, but she could feel him.

Feel every part of him.

His long fingers spanned her ribs, holding her lower body up off the bed. He knelt between her legs, forcing her thighs apart, splaying her wide open for him. With her feet bouncing awkwardly and her stomach muscles stretched taut, it wasn't the most comfortable of positions.

Riana didn't care.

She clung to the worn bedding above her head and futilely struggled to free herself from his viselike grip so she could pump her hips against the hard, fast thrusting of his cock. Her helplessness only intensified the frantic pressure building at her center, and the moans she'd been making earlier transformed into little sobs of pleasure.

Cain made a guttural sound in the dark, but there wasn't enough light to see his expression. He'd awakened her a few minutes ago by rubbing his erection against her butt.

After a month of sharing this cell with him, her body immediately responded to the silent invitation.

Now she was naked on her back, her bottom several inches off the mattress, her pussy wet and aching with sharp, deep desire for him.

"Oh, oh God!" Her voice was shrill and breathless and louder than she'd expected. But the urgency of her growing climax made it impossible for her to stifle her vocal responses.

Cain grunted in response, the sound of his breathing intensifying as his fingers tightened on her ribs. He almost never spoke while he fucked her, but by now she could read his grunt as one of approval.

He liked it when she was loud, when the pleasure was too much for her to control.

Riana clawed at the mattress and bit down hard on her lower lip, but it was no use. Her choked cries grew even louder, echoing in the complete darkness and nearly drowning the sound of wet suction from his cock inside her and the choppy tempo of the slapping of their groins. "So good. Oh fuck!"

Cain made another rough grunt, adjusting his hold on her so he could thrust even faster and harder.

She was washed in heat and perspiration, and her blindness in the dark only increased her helplessness against the overwhelming sensations.

"Make me come." She arched her back desperately in an attempt to grind her pussy against his pumping.

"Yeah," Cain gritted out, the unexpected words shaped without warning, his low, thick voice the most erotic thing she'd ever heard. "Come for me hard."

She came. Hard. The climax sliced through her so powerfully she nearly screamed as she shook and shuddered through the spasms.

He kept fucking her through the clenching of her pussy, pushing into her with several rough groans as his body tightened palpably. "Again," he demanded in a strangled tone, still holding her body rigidly in place.

She didn't know if it was the rough, irresistible authority in his voice or the intensity of the carnal sensations. But she came again, the second climax rising up on the heels of the first, making her cry out even louder as the pleasure erupted once more.

Cain didn't shout as he came. But he forced out a choked exclamation she recognized as the one he made when he came particularly hard. Then his body jerked and pulsed with his climax, and his hands finally relaxed on her ribs.

"Shut the fuck up!" someone yelled from outside the cell. In the disorientation of such complete darkness, she couldn't even tell from which direction the annoyed shout had come.

Riana giggled as Cain released her, and she stretched out to try to ease her tight muscles. She'd become accustomed to the lack of privacy far sooner than she would have expected. She was occasionally hit with self-consciousness—if one of the other prisoners caught her in an unusual position. The other day she'd been fucking Cain as he'd sat on the edge of the bed, leaning back on his arms. She was on his lap, facing away from him, her legs folded beside his thighs, bracing herself on his knees and bouncing on his cock as frantically as she could. She'd been naked, her breasts jiggling wildly, while Cain had held himself perfectly still. She'd come three times, riding him with shameless eagerness. For some reason when she'd noticed there was an audience of several gawking prisoners, she'd burned with mortification—although she'd come a fourth time, knowing she was being watched.

But usually she could shrug off the lack of privacy.

It was amazing what familiarity could accomplish.

Cain collapsed beside her, breathing heavily and stretching out beside her. He didn't reach out to pull her against him. He wasn't the cuddling kind. But she felt his eyes on her in the dark.

"I suppose you're pretty proud of yourself," she said in a dry voice.

He grunted. A sound she understood as agreement.

"I just screamed to feed your enormous ego," she lied. "I thought you needed some encouragement."

He grunted again. This one sounded amused.

"It wasn't that good," she continued, pleased with her success. Cain wasn't an open or easy man, and it always gave her a thrill when she managed to connect with him in a way other than sex. "But you're making good strides. Keep at it, and I'm sure you'll get better."

Her teasing got a more dramatic reaction than she'd expected. Cain rolled over on top of her—hot, heavy, and damp with perspiration. She could feel his warm breath against her flushed cheek and—although she still couldn't see his expression only inches away from her—she could sense his predatory smile in the dark.

He adjusted until he could slip one hand down between her thighs. His fingers explored her groin, stroking the hot, swollen flesh and her pussy, sloppy and wet from his fluids and hers. "Is that right?" he said, the gravel in his voice making her shiver.

"Yes." She tensed as she felt his thumb close over her sensitized clit, but she managed to say in a somewhat wry voice, "Don't be discouraged. You're still learning."

He lowered his face until he could murmur in her ear, "How's this for a lesson?"

Then he began to rub her clit in firm circles with his thumb.

She tried to resist—willing herself to keep control of her reactions so she could keep the upper hand in their teasing conversation.

But it was no use. Her body was already overly stimulated, and now it was primed and ready for his touch.

It took less than a minute of his massage for another climax to coil and release inside her. She bit down hard on his shoulder to keep herself from choking out the pleasure that pulsed through her.

"Forty-seven seconds," he drawled, stroking her pussy as the lingering spasms died away.

"Arrogant bastard," she replied without any heat. "That one was fake too."

He actually laughed—a low, throaty sound she almost never heard from him.

She experienced a flush of pleasure at the sound.

He was so hard to figure out, and she had no idea how he felt about her.

She knew he loved to fuck her—she had ample proof of that—but that might be because she was the only available, willing female in his present circumstances. They fucked a lot, sometimes three or four times a day. But they didn't have much else to do, and at least it was an enjoyable way to pass the time.

She knew he tolerated her pretty well. She did her best to make herself accommodating—even when he was silent and bad-tempered. She tried to be helpful and interesting and did her best to be a good companion.

But she didn't know if he actually liked her. If he had feelings for her beyond lust and easy tolerance.

And she wanted Cain to like her. Desperately.

So much she thrilled at every small sign that he might.

She supposed it wasn't entirely healthy. She'd latched onto him with unnatural neediness since there was absolutely no one else to bond with in the hell where she was living. Under normal circumstances, she might not have even liked him. Much less developed so strong an attachment to this rough, silent loner.

But she spent a good portion of her endless days brooding about Cain, wondering what made him tick, dissecting every comment he made to her, and hoping she was growing on him too.

Sometimes she daydreamed about escaping the prison, and in those daydreams she and Cain always left together.

And they stayed together even after they were freed.

Other times she had nightmares about a freak accident occurring and Cain getting killed. Her horror in those imaginings wasn't just about what would happen to her. It was also about losing Cain.

Most of the time she tried not to think about either of those things. She tried to just live in the moment since anything else was almost unbearable.

Right now she wanted to roll over and snuggle with Cain. She wanted him to put his arms around her and hold her close. She didn't make a move though. The last thing she wanted to do was make Cain feel uncomfortable about anything connected to sex.

Sex was all she had, and it was the only thing keeping her safe.

When the lights came back on in the Hold, Cain rolled out of bed and headed to the bathroom—just as he always did. She stayed under the covers. Other prisoners often strolled by Cain's cell first thing in the morning, hoping to catch a glimpse of her cleaning up or getting dressed. Because of this, she always waited until the early meal, when Cain left to get them food, to clean up as best she could.

There was only so clean she could get here, but she did what she could—grateful she at least had use of a sink.

She washed out her clothes as often as possible although she had to be careful since they were already getting threadbare and stained. Despite her attempts to stay clean, she knew she must smell a lot of the time. After the first week, however, she'd stopped letting that bother her.

Her own senses had grown accustomed to the smell of the Hold. So much so that she hardly noticed it anymore, unless she got close to a particularly reeking man. Cain had a distinct smell. One she actually liked now since it had grown so familiar to her.

She kind of hoped he felt the same way about how she smelled. They had sex so often she sometimes wondered if most of the time she smelled like Cain anyway.

Her hair was basically hopeless. Cain had found her something that resembled a comb, and she spent hours trying to work it through her snarled mass of dark hair. She washed her hair in the sink sometimes, but there was no soap or shampoo. She'd given up hoping that her hair would ever look attractive again.

Cain had offered to shave it off for her—the way he shaved his own scalp with the blade he kept hidden behind the toilet. But Riana couldn't yet bring herself to give up her hair completely.

Maybe later she would get there. But not yet.

She had let Cain shave her pussy. Two weeks ago. Initially it had been for purely practical reasons, but the act had ended up being intensely erotic. And when he'd finished the delicate procedure, he'd had her hold herself open intimately so he could pleasure her with his lips, tongue, and teeth.

She'd come three times—the last time screaming.

Just the memory of it still made her wet.

Since Cain had left for the morning mealtime, Riana got up to go to the bathroom and get washed up.

She'd never actually seen the mealtime madness since it went on beyond the sight of the cell, and she had no desire to do so. She had taken to observing people during the downtimes, more than she'd done at the beginning, whenever there weren't men hanging about the bars to ogle.

She'd never grown fully inured to violence, so there were some things she just couldn't look at, but occasionally it was quiet enough for her to look through the bars and observe life in the Hold.

She grew to recognize certain people—even though she never learned their names. There was one elderly man who seemed to spend all day making slow laps around the prison, darting out of the way of anyone who looked like a threat. He must have lived on scraps since he never participated in the mealtime rush. She mentally christened him the Tortoise. Another guy must have been a kleptomaniac since she would often see him snatching things that belonged to others—not with brute force the way the alphas did but with quick, covert movements as if he just couldn't help it. He would sometimes get beat up, but he never stole anything important enough to get killed over. She called him the Snatcher.

Then there was the Player. He'd arrived just over a week ago. She'd noticed him immediately because he was very good-looking. He wore expensive clothes, and he walked with a kind of swagger that made it clear he was used to getting what he wanted. He was definitely a ladies' man, which was why she'd named him the Player.

She'd expected him to be dead before the first night was over since his clothes were so much better than anyone else's and because there were men here who would take his confidence as defiance.

She'd been shocked when she continued to see him— still in his clothes, never beat up. Then he claimed his own cell—not a good one but better than nothing—and no one tried to take it from him. He was in good shape but in a lean way. He wasn't nearly as big as Cain or Thorn. There was no way he could have taken on some of the men here through brute strength.

She wondered how he was surviving. His cell was across from hers and Cain's, and no one seemed to bother him. He didn't appear to have made friends or alliances or given himself as a lover to an alpha who could protect him.

Because she was so curious, she would sometimes watch him when she was alone in the cell and he was in her range of view.

He was an anomaly. He didn't make sense.

This morning, the Player hadn't gone for food in the rush. He didn't always although he clearly managed to eat enough to stay healthy. It seemed more like he couldn't always be bothered. Right now he was in his cell, sitting on his bed, leaning against the wall with his eyes closed.

As if he'd sensed her watching, he opened his eyes and met her gaze across the distance.

This guy wasn't like most of the other animals in the Hold, but she had no idea who or what he was.

After a minute, he got up and walked toward her.

When he reached the bars of the cell, he gave her a breathtaking grin, one that literally made her breath hitch. "I don't suppose you can spare one of those blankets."

She found herself reaching down for one automatically before she caught herself. What the hell? So he had a good smile—that didn't mean she lost her mind over him. "I don't think he would like that."

She never spoke Cain's name where anyone else could hear it. He'd given it to her as a gesture of goodwill. He hadn't given it to anyone else.

"Probably not. But would he even notice?" Again the man was so charming and persuasive that she wanted to just cave and give him what he wanted.

"Yes. He would."

"What has he done to deserve such loyalty?" This seemed more like a genuine question rather than a ploy to persuade her.

She met his gaze evenly, noticing his eyes were a remarkably vivid green. "What do you think?"

He sighed. "Best cell. Best woman. I might be jealous."

Cain had told her how he'd taken this cell from the prisoner who'd had it when he arrived. The man had been strong—so strong Cain had been seriously injured after the fight—but Cain had beaten him and taken the key. He'd die before he gave it up now.

She said, "I wouldn't challenge him if I were you."

The Player laughed. "I'm way too smart for that."

He probably was. Maybe that was how he'd survived as long as he did. Some sort of razor-sharp intelligence and the ability to persuade people to take his side.

It had worked on her—so easily it was almost frightening. This man might look more like a player than a warrior, but there was something dangerous about him all the same.

She was about to reply when Cain appeared out of nowhere. He swung a blow toward the other man, but the Player ducked out of the range of Cain's fist just in time.

He was really quick—that was for sure.

"Get away," Cain muttered, aiming an intimidating glare in his direction.

The man backed off, but he gave Riana a shameless wink in the process that made Cain growl.

She wanted to laugh. She really wanted to laugh. Who the hell was that guy anyway?

"What was he doing?" Cain demanded, entering the cell and locking it behind him.

"Just talking. I think he was bored."

"Stay away from him. There's something not right about him."

"What do you mean?" She'd sensed something strange too, but she wondered if Cain had a better take on it. "What's not right?"

"I don't know. I've heard rumblings though. No one will challenge him."

"Why don't you?"

"Not worth my time." He gave Riana a significant look. "Unless he tries to take what's mine."

She swallowed, feeling a little turned on by the words, but she managed to say, "Well, I protected your blankets for you, so I think they're safe."

That earned her an almost-smile.

When Cain gave her the food he'd brought back, Riana accepted her portion with thanks. She'd never gone with him to retrieve the meals. Cain wouldn't have been able to concentrate on protecting her as well as claiming food for both of them. So he always left her locked in the cell, and Riana had never complained.

She didn't complain about anything anyway. Even things that genuinely bugged her. She kept all her annoyances—the inevitable result of living in such close quarters with a terse, stoic man—to herself.

She had no idea how many complaints it would take for Cain to get sick of her and banish her from his cell, but she wasn't about to test his limits.

The meal always consisted of stew and bread, and sometimes Riana could barely swallow it because she was so tired of the stuff. But Cain always got grumpy and disapproving when she didn't eat—the way he acted whenever she showed signs of not being tough enough—so she usually managed to force down enough to keep herself full.

She'd started working out with Cain—doing as many push-ups and sit-ups as she could and running at least a couple of laps around the perimeter of the Hold with him until she was too exhausted to keep up. He would lock her in the cell when she'd done all she could, and he would finish his run by himself.

Some mornings he ran for hours.

In the afternoons he would work on building his device. She still had no idea what it was, although she could now see how parts of it functioned and was pretty sure it would end up being some kind of primitive machine. There was absolutely nothing for her to do, so she would watch him until she dozed off.

If he was in an amiable mood—or what passed for amiable for Cain—they would talk as he worked. She told him about her childhood and her grandmother, the only person she'd ever really loved. And she told him about her schooling, her job, and the various digs she'd gone on over the years, how alone she'd been for most of her life.

Cain didn't tell her nearly as much. He wasn't an open or talkative person. But he told her about some of the trips he'd made—he'd traveled all over Coalition space. And once he told her about his dog.

Max.

It was the only time in the month she'd known him Riana had seen something like grief on his face.

At some point in the afternoons, Cain usually went on the "hunt" for some object he needed for his device. Riana always went with him—mostly to get out of the cell for a little while.

This afternoon, when Cain got up from the floor where he'd been tinkering on his machine, Riana jumped to her feet immediately. She was restless today. Cain had been silent and brooding, and they hadn't had sex since before the lights had come on. She'd washed out her camisole and hung it up to drip dry, but that was all she'd accomplished all day.

She needed to do something.

Cain didn't question her joining him. He was used to it by now. In fact, he didn't say anything as he locked the door behind him.

Sometimes when they returned, a prisoner was trying to break into the cell—either by force or by jimmying the lock. Cain usually just swatted them out of the way. It was always an act of hopeless desperation since there was no way to get into the cell without the key. The bars were utterly impassable.

They started walking around the Hold, and Cain was clearly on the lookout for whatever it was he needed today. When they passed by a scuffle—evidently over a pair of shoes—Cain eased her toward the wall so she wouldn't get struck with a stray blow.

She was forced so close to the wall that her shirt caught on a jagged edge of metal.

It tore, the fabric ripping at one of the seams so far that the gap exposed her bare breast.

Her camisole was still in the cell drying.

"Damn it," she muttered, holding the torn fabric in place as a few prisoners who happened to see hooted or called out vulgar comments. When she realized the implications of the accident—one of her few pieces of clothing was permanently damaged—she felt vaguely sick. "Fuck, fuck, damn it."

Cain had stopped when she did, but his expression looked mostly unconcerned. "It's just a tear."

Her teeth snapped together as she managed to hold back an automatic retort. It wasn't just a tear. Not in these circumstances. And any idiot would have known that.

She couldn't comfortably keep holding up the torn fabric of her shirt, so with a defeated sigh, she said, "I guess I need to go back."

"Why?"

Riana's lower lip dropped slightly. "What do you mean—why? Because I have a gaping hole in my shirt, and I'm not going to walk around half-naked."

Cain looked slightly impatient and gave a shrug with one shoulder. "What's the big deal? They've seen you naked in the cell before. They've seen you with my cock in your mouth. What's the difference?"

A flash of outraged anger overcame her as she stared at his infuriating face. There was a world of difference between the two situations. Yes, some of the other prisoners had seen her in various states of undress and debauchery, but that had all been in the cell. The cell felt like home base. It might not be private, but it was safe.

It was entirely different to parade around the Hold, revealing her body to every prisoner with eyes.

And if Cain had the slightest bit of sensitivity in his brute soul, he would know it.

She could see a glimpse of Thorn from where they stood. Thorn kept his distance from Cain now, but he'd managed to hold on to his power in the prison otherwise. Riana tried very hard not to encounter him since just the sight of him made her feel kind of sick.

And even Thorn could ogle her now with the torn shirt.

"Of course it's different," she snapped. "What the fuck do you—"

She broke off her words with a jerk, belatedly remembering that she couldn't make Cain mad.

Swallowing hard, she overcame the urge to bite his head off and instead said, "You're right. There's no difference." Her eyes straight ahead, she let the tear in her shirt fall open and started walking again.

Without warning, Cain grabbed her arm and swung her around to face him. "Why the hell do you do that?"

Surprised by his burst of anger, Riana gasped, "Do what?"

"Cut yourself off whenever you have something to say." His blue eyes pinned her in place, and his jaw was clenched with obvious tension. "It drives me crazy. If you have something to say, just say it. Don't act like a mindless, passive drone."

For a moment, her vision blurred over—she was so enraged and affronted. Her hands fisted at her sides as she tried to keep herself from clawing lines down his face. "Why the fuck do you think I stop myself! Do you actually expect me to challenge you when you're the only thing keeping me alive?"

Something on his face changed. It didn't soften. She'd never seen Cain soft. Instead, his features tightened even more until his lips were pressed into a colorless line. Finally he rasped, "You think if you say the wrong thing I'm going to toss you out to be torn apart?"

"What am I supposed to think?" All the suppressed frustration of constantly being on edge for the past month was finally boiling over. Her voice was hoarse with emotion too fiery and thick to control. "That's our arrangement. You protect me. I please you. We've never said it out loud, but both of us know it. I'm sure as hell not going to *displease* you."

His eyes cut into her like a blade. "You think I'm that kind of an animal?"

"Of course you're that kind of animal. We all are. Look around you!" She made a sweeping gesture, taking in the Hold, the dirty chaos around them, the primitive way all the prisoners lived in this cage. "We eat and fuck and try to survive. That's what we've been turned into. What the fuck do you expect me to do to?" Her voice faltered suddenly, overcome with a terror so deep it almost swallowed her. She might have killed herself here—by finally expressing what she thought. Lashing out at the one man who was capable of keeping her safe. She made a choking sound and looked at the ground. "I'm just trying to survive."

Cain was silent. But she could feel the shuddering tension in his hard, muscular body, even though he wasn't touching her. She could also hear him breathe. Loud, fast, wet, thick sounds of inhales and exhales.

She finally darted her eyes up to his face as she tried to keep her hands from trembling.

She'd never seen Cain truly angry before.

But he was angry now.

He was smoldering with it. Shaking with it. Like a volcano about to erupt.

And he was angry with *her.*

Cain took a loud ragged breath and turned on his heel, away from her. He didn't move. Instead, he stood with his back to her and simmered, as if he were struggling to get himself under control.

Riana stared at his broad back, the rippling muscles of his shoulders and arms, the way his T-shirt stuck to his damp skin, the distinct curve of his scalp.

And her terror almost swallowed her up.

What if, because of her own stupidity, she'd lost Cain for good?

She could hardly breathe, and she suddenly needed to get away. Back to the cell where she felt safe.

With a muffled sound, she turned back in the direction they'd come and stumbled away. She wasn't thinking rationally. It was pure instinct driving her to escape. Had she been thinking, she would have remembered that the cell was locked and she didn't have a key.

Despite her emotional state, she never once believed she was seriously in danger of being assaulted. Everyone knew she was Cain's woman. And everyone was scared or intimidated by Cain. Just last week, when a man had tried to cop a quick feel during their morning run, Cain had beaten the man unconscious—in the presence of the entire Hold.

Even apart from him, she still considered herself under his protection.

Which was why she was completely unprepared when someone suddenly grabbed her and pulled her into a dim cell without bars.

It happened so quickly she could barely process it. One moment she was stumbling toward her cell and the next she was being thrown violently against a wall.

The impact hurt. It winded and jarred her so much she was too dizzy to react. Her assailant didn't waste any time. He hauled her up roughly from the floor and then pushed her forward, forcing her to bend over the edge of a metal table. It was the same kind of table as the one in Cain's cell—small and attached to the wall.

The attack was so fast and brutal that Riana couldn't even tell who the man was. A forceful hand closed around the back of her neck, holding her in place on the table with so strong a grip she could barely even breathe.

She tried to scream but no sound came out. Either fear or the strangling grip on her neck made any noise impossible. She tried to struggle, but she was helpless in this position, folded and pinned over the edge of the table.

Her consciousness glazed over in a blur of terror and shock. One part of her mind knew what was happening, but the rest of it couldn't even register the reality.

A brutish hand jerked down her pants and panties until she felt the cold metal against her bare skin.

She tried to scream again. And it was the worst part of the whole experience. Her mouth opened but couldn't shape any sound at all.

With what was left of her mind, she tried to prepare herself for what was going to occur even as she futilely kept trying to struggle against the powerful grip.

Then suddenly the hands were gone. She heard a primal growling sound, and the body behind her was pulled away.

She sucked in a desperate breath through her aching windpipe as she managed to push her bruised body off the table so she could see what was happening.

Cain had found her.

He must have torn the man off her and thrown him bodily out of the cell and into the public area in the middle of the Hold.

Riana now recognized her attacker as Asp, the tattooed man who'd confronted her on her first arrival.

But she could hardly recognize Cain at all in the snarling, primitive beast he seemed to have transformed into.

She managed to pull up her pants before she stepped, shaking, out of the cell and huddled by the wall as she watched.

Asp wasn't a weakling. He was big and violent, and he knew what he was doing.

But he didn't have a chance against Cain.

Cain had worked himself up into a frenzy. Riana had never seem him—seen anyone—look like that before. He pounded the other man into the ground, never pausing or giving respite for a moment. Soon there was blood. And then the other man stopped putting up a fight.

But Cain didn't stop his brutal attack until Asp lay in a mass of bloody pulp on the ground.

Riana knew without doubt he was dead.

And she wasn't even sorry. Part of her was shocked and nauseated by the sudden, violent turn of events over the past few minutes. But part of her—a tiny, instinctive part she didn't like to acknowledge—thrilled to see Cain react so primally, so territorially, so animalistically.

Over her.

Mostly, though, she was dizzy and dazed—too much having happened for her to keep up.

So when Cain dropped the other man to the ground and stood up with his hands, arms, and shirt bloodied and his skin soaked with grimy perspiration, she still couldn't bring herself to move.

Cain looked around the prison. The whole place had grown silent as everyone had moved to watch the violent altercation. Cain's expression seemed to dare anyone else to challenge him.

Or to lay a hand on what was his.

No one moved. No one dared to approach.

Until Cain finally stalked away from his kill.

When he reached Riana, he took her by the back of her torn shirt and used his grip to guide her back to their cell.

His touch wasn't gentle, and it smeared blood on her shirt, but she appreciated the support since she wasn't sure she would have been able to walk otherwise.

When they reached the cell and Cain locked the door behind them, Riana crumpled onto the bed, hugging her arms to her stomach.

Cain stared down at her for a moment. Then he made a guttural sound and jerked away. He strode to the sink and turned the water on. He splashed water on his bloody hands and sweaty face.

Water streaming down his skin, he turned back toward her. "Did he—"

"No," she gasped, the first word she'd been able to utter since the attack. "You got there in time."

His face twisted strangely, and he turned back to the sink. Leaned down to splash more water on his face.

He turned back toward her—still looking feral and powerful in his visceral tension and bloody shirt—and opened his mouth again. But this time he didn't speak. Instead, he turned on his heel with a jerk and made a move like he was going to leave the cell.

But he stopped himself. And instead he moved back to where she was huddled on the bed.

But he stopped himself again.

Riana had no idea what was happening, but she could sense Cain's mood. Adrenaline and testosterone must be coursing through him. He was still on the violent high. Plus he might be concerned about her.

And he had no idea how to channel his primitive response.

He splashed more water on his face. Then he made another guttural sound and paced into the bathroom nook.

Growing concerned now, Riana stood up and met him as he turned back around and walked out.

"Cain, are you all right?" she asked softly, stretching out a gentle hand toward his stained shirt.

She was engulfed by the oddest feeling. Her own fear and nausea had dissipated in the security of the cell, and in its wake was a primal urge that matched his.

She felt all physicality and instinct. Like an animal.

An animal that had just been claimed by its mate.

At her soft touch, Cain's battered control broke completely. And as if he'd read her mind, he growled softly and grabbed her by the hips.

He pushed her back against the wall of the cell and claimed her mouth in a hard, rough, urgent kiss.

It was the first time he'd ever kissed her, and Riana responded to it immediately. She still wasn't thinking rationally, but the horror of the minutes before was mostly gone—with only animal instinct remaining.

She wanted Cain. She wanted his strength and his power and his dominance. She needed to feel all those things in the most physical way she could.

His body pressed into hers, trapping her against the hard wall. His hands were all over her—feeling her, touching her, stroking her—until he'd pulled off her pants and panties in their haze of frantic need.

With powerful hands, Cain lifted her up then, using the wall for support as he held her bare bottom. She wrapped her legs around his middle and clung to his neck. He was strong enough to hold her easily, and she loved how small and feminine she felt against him.

He didn't waste any time. As soon as he'd fumbled between their bodies to free his cock, he sank into her. She wasn't as wet as she usually was—the panic earlier was still having an effect on her body—but she wanted him. Needed him. Desperately.

His cock filled her completely, and he pitched his hips forward, pushing into her, pushing her hard against the wall.

It wasn't entirely comfortable, and Riana was conscious of sore places on her body where there would be bruises from the earlier attack, but she didn't care. She wanted to feel Cain's strength as deeply as she could.

He didn't have much control. His thrusts were hard and erratic, and his mouth on hers was clumsy and ravenous. But it was exactly what Riana needed. And she whimpered in pleasure as he rutted, as he took her hard, as he claimed her as his.

She clawed eager lines down the back of his neck as he grunted roughly and rocked his pelvis into hers.

She wasn't going to come. She hadn't had enough clitoral stimulation, and the earlier episode kept her from concentrating enough to reach orgasm.

But she didn't care.

Feeling Cain this way, watching him release all his shuddering tension in her at last, holding on to his absolute strength and masculinity, was the hottest thing she'd ever known.

She squeezed her pussy around the penetration of his cock until he jerked his head to the side and held himself still. Then he made a sound like a muted roar and jerked his hips in fast, clumsy spasms until he released himself inside her.

They were both gasping desperately as Cain's body started to relax at last. Carefully he pulled back from the wall, helped her untangle her legs, and set her down on the floor.

Her knees buckled immediately, so he picked her up instead and carried her over to the bed.

She curled up in a ball, feeling oddly weak and uncertain now that the surge of adrenalin and emotion had passed.

She desperately wanted Cain to hold her, but he didn't get onto the bed with her. Instead, he went over to the sink and picked up one of the threadbare towels. After dampening it with the water, he came back over and sat down on the edge of the mattress.

When he'd gently uncurled her body, he removed the torn remnants of her shirt—now stained with the blood from his chest—and then wiped off the smears of blood from her skin.

She watched him in astonishment, her lips slightly parted and her eyes wide and round. He didn't meet her eyes. Instead, he focused on his hand as he stroked the damp cloth over her breasts and belly and then down farther to her pussy—where he cleaned up his semen.

Riana had never seen him like this before, and the silent care made her belly knot with a nameless emotion she was too afraid to put into words.

"Thank you," she said at last.

He jerked slightly, wincing as if she'd struck him.

"What's wrong?" She put a hand on his arm, afraid he might pull back.

"Don't—" He stopped abruptly and cleared his throat. "I'm sorry."

Really confused now—and even more confused when she saw the twisting of regret on his face—she tightened her fingers on his forearm. "What are you sorry for?"

His eyes finally met hers. "For just now. I shouldn't have… You were almost raped, and I… I took you like that—without even letting you recover."

"Oh." Her heart hammered wildly, and her breath kept hitching in her throat. "But I…"

He was caught up in a guilt she'd never expected to see from him. "I don't know what got into me." He stared down at his hands, which were clenched in his lap. "I was like an…"

An animal. So was she.

"I didn't even ask if you wanted it." With a ragged breath, he shifted his eyes to meet hers again.

"I did want it," she said, her voice breaking on the second word. "I did. I would have stopped you if I didn't."

Cain stared at her for a long time. "And you believe I would have stopped if you'd told me to."

"Of course you would. You aren't like them." She made a weak gesture out to the rest of the prison. "I know I said you were before. But you aren't."

He finally let out his breath and got up to put the towel in the sink.

Then to her absolute relief, he came back over and lowered himself into bed beside her. He rolled over onto his side and spooned her from behind. He wrapped his arms around her, exactly as she wanted, needed him to.

Riana almost choked on emotion as she snuggled back against him—feeling safe and comforted despite the incongruous circumstances.

"Are you all right?" he muttered against her ear, his arms tightening around her middle as if he were unconsciously still trying to protect her.

"Yeah." She adjusted one of his forearms so she could hug it to her chest. "I'm just now fully processing what might have happened. It all happened so quickly. I still can't really believe it."

He was silent, except for his warm, heavy breathing against her hair.

"Thank you," she whispered. "For stopping him."

"I should have been there sooner. I was looking for you but couldn't find you for a minute. I never should have turned my back on you out there."

She could hear the lingering guilt in his voice, and that sign of his humanity comforted her almost as much as his strong arms. "It's not your fault. I'm the one who walked away from you. I wasn't thinking."

He didn't reply for a minute, just held her so close it was almost uncomfortable. Finally he asked, "Why didn't you scream? Didn't you think I would come for you?"

Riana sucked in a sharp breath at the implications. "I knew you would. I tried. I just… I just couldn't get my throat to work."

As she remembered the horrifying experience, a shuddering sob escaped her throat. "It was terrible."

Cain made a rough sound—as if he were wordlessly objecting to her crying.

She shook helplessly for a minute. Not really weeping but finally releasing the emotional tension.

When she got herself under control again, she rasped, "I hate this place."

Cain tightened his arms around her again and said against her hair, "I know."

They lay in silence for a long time, and Riana had no desire to leave the haven that his embrace provided her.

Eventually she noticed a faint smear of blood on the bedding, and it made her remember something else. Still hugging his forearm to her chest, she asked softly, "Are you all right?"

He tensed up slightly behind her. "What do you mean?"

It was a risk. This morning she never would have taken it. But she did now. She explained, "You killed a man just now."

The pause was long and tense. But Cain finally answered in a thick voice, "I know. I don't regret it."

"Me either," she admitted although it was strangely hard for her to say. "But still. I thought maybe it might be… hard."

She'd never killed anyone so she didn't know how it would feel. For all she knew, Cain might have killed dozens of men. He might be a serial killer.

But she didn't really think so. And she couldn't help but wonder how he felt about having beaten a man to death the way he had.

He didn't reply for a really long time. Just kept holding her and breathing into her hair. He was silent for so long she assumed he wasn't going to respond, and she didn't blame him at all.

But then finally he murmured, so low she could barely hear it, "I hate this place too."

The next day, when Cain was gone for the morning food rush, the Player from the opposite cell stopped by in front of the bars. He'd been walking around and must have noticed she was alone. Evidently, Cain's warning to stay away hadn't sunk in.

"Do you need anything?" he asked, looking almost serious for once. He was classically handsome, but he didn't have a young man's prettiness. He must be in his thirties, and there was a slight roughness to his appearance that testified to hard experience and made him even more attractive.

"I have someone to give me what I need," she said coolly, wanting to make sure not to give him any encouragement. He was definitely different from most of the prisoners—he'd somehow managed to hold on to his civilization—but she was Cain's woman, and she wanted there to be no mistake about that.

"Yeah. I've noticed that. After yesterday, I mean. Are you okay?"

He must have either heard or seen what happened with Asp.

She nodded. "Yeah. I had protection." Then she added because he looked genuinely concerned, "He got there in time."

The man's face relaxed.

He'd only been here a short time. She wondered if he'd eventually turn hard and ruthless and primitive like most of the other prisoners here.

"What is he making there?" the man asked, nodding toward Cain's device.

Riana didn't answer that question.

"If he's got some sort of escape plan, let me know. I could definitely help."

The words should have been presumptuous since he was a stranger to her, but she actually believed him. He wasn't putting on that persuasive act like he had before. It felt like he was telling her the truth.

And she wondered if he could. There was something about this man that felt like lurking power, danger—although not directed at her.

"Who are you?" she blurted out.

He laughed, a warm, genuine sound rarely heard in the prison. "My name is Hall."

"And what do you do?"

"I'm a freelancer."

"What kind of freelancing?"

"A variety of jobs that pay well."

That felt about right for the way she'd sized him up. "What jobs?"

"Whatever. I'm good at a lot. It's the payment I care about."

"What did you do to end up here?"

He opened his mouth to answer, but he never did. Cain had appeared behind him and reached out to shove him away from the bars.

Hall must have reacted instinctively. He swung his arms up into a fighter's pose, and then he caught Cain's fist before it slammed into his face.

There was no way Hall was strong enough to resist the strength of Cain's blow, but for some reason Cain's arm stopped before it reached its target.

Cain stared, looking blank for a minute.

Hall was stepping back with a smile. "I didn't mean to intrude," he said, calling on what must be his natural instinct for self-preservation.

Then Cain suddenly acted. So quickly Riana could barely keep up. One minute the two men were several feet apart, and then suddenly Cain had grabbed Hall and thrown him up against the bars of the cell, holding him in place with his forearm against Hall's throat.

"What did you just do?" Cain gritted out through clenched teeth.

Riana jumped out of the bed. "He wasn't doing anything," she said hurriedly. "He was just talking. He wasn't offensive."

She didn't mind Cain clearing the path for them with force, but Hall hadn't done anything to deserve this kind of violence.

Cain's eyes never left Hall's face. "What did you do to me just now?"

Riana realized he was asking something different, and her heart started to race even more.

"Nothing," Hall said, not resisting the force in any way. "I was just protecting myself. Sorry if I got in the way."

Riana somehow knew the man wasn't a coward. He was smart. He only picked the fights he knew he could win, and he must not be sure he could win out against Cain.

"Tell me what you did to me, or I'll crush your windpipe."

Something loosened in Hall's body, and he said hoarsely, "I'm a Reader."

Riana made a little noise of surprise, and even Cain straightened up.

The Coalition had rounded up all the Readers about a decade ago. They'd forced them all to work for the government and were now controlling their reproduction, so Readers were supposed to have vanished from the general population.

"You weren't just Reading me a minute ago," Cain muttered, his arm still at the other man's throat. "I felt you do something."

"My gift takes a slightly different form. I can read other people's feelings when I touch them. What I can pick up is a lot vaguer than other Readers, but I can turn it around too. I can use what I sense, turn it around, and send it back. That's what I did to you."

"Why are you telling me this?" Cain asked, looking predatory, suspicious.

Hall gave a quirk of a smile. "Because you asked?"

"He wasn't doing any harm," Riana said quietly. Hall seemed like a real person to her now—and she thought he would to Cain too. If Cain killed him, it would just be wrong, and she didn't want Cain to have to live with that. "He was just defending himself."

Cain hesitated, obviously torn. Then he finally let Hall go. Hall shook himself off and straightened up, somehow maintaining the look of amused superiority.

"Stay away from both of us," Cain growled.

Hall arched his eyebrows at Riana in some sort of unspoken communication. "Got it." Then he turned around and left.

Cain was tense and silent when he entered the cell and locked it behind him.

He was bristling, and she knew he was troubled by what had just happened with Hall.

"He really wasn't being offensive," she said, trying to break the tension. Hall made more sense to her now. She could see how he'd managed to carve out a place for himself here, and she could understand why he was so persuasive.

"So now you're defending him?" Cain's words cut like a knife.

"No! I just think he's not that important, so there's no reason to get uptight about it. Why has he gotten to you like this?"

Cain narrowed his eyes and glared at her, not answering.

She was so annoyed she wanted to shake him. "What the hell is your problem? Do you think I'm considering moving out of your cell and into his?"

She asked the final question mostly to get a reaction, to snap him out of his bristling. Not because she thought it was true.

But she saw a flicker of something in his eyes and suddenly realized it *was*. He thought she liked Hall—better than him. He thought she might be wondering if he were a better choice for a mate.

"Oh my God, Cain," she groaned, dropping down to sit on the edge of the bed. "How could you possibly think that?"

He didn't answer. Just stood over her, staring down, something both angry and hesitant on his face.

"I chose *you*. I live with you, fuck you, depend on you completely. Damn it, I even smell like you. How could you possibly think I'd change my mind and choose someone else?"

He still didn't answer. Not with words. But something seemed to have cracked inside him, because he was suddenly on top of her, pushing her down so she was lying on her back.

He kissed her hard, possessive, and her whole body and soul answered his claim. She arched up into him, clawing at the back of his neck,

Soon he'd pulled off her pants and pulled out his cock, and he was entering her with rough thrusts.

She was totally overwhelmed with his strength, his power, his possession. Even without much foreplay, she was aching with arousal, her hips eagerly grinding against his thrusts.

She could barely breathe around the depth of the kiss, but he didn't break it until they'd worked up a rough, rhythmic motion. Then finally he tore his mouth away and said thickly, "Tell me you're mine."

"I'm yours," she gasped, meaning it—far more than in body. "Just yours."

She came on the last word, pleasure rippling through her, and Cain stifled an exclamation of satisfaction as he let himself go too.

He fell down on top of her afterward, gathering her into his arms.

And she loved it—all of how he felt and looked and sounded and smelled as he held her.

She understood why he'd needed to assure himself that she was his woman, but she couldn't help but wish the situation was mutual.

That he was hers—fully, for real—too.

That evening after mealtime Cain worked on his device again. He wasn't just tinkering now. He seemed driven, concentrating so hard on his work that he was barely conscious of her presence.

She wondered if he was close to finishing it.

She wondered what it was going to do.

She wondered if it would be what he wanted it to be—an escape out of this misery.

When he finally put down his tool and covered the device with the sheet again, his expression looked blank and unfocused.

She sat up in bed and hugged her arms to her chest. "Cain," she began, her voice weak and shaky, "when you get out of here, when you escape, please don't leave me behind."

FOUR

Time passed strangely in the Hold.

Each day seemed to drag on forever, but the string of days—one after the other, each exactly alike—would disappear in the blink of an eye.

Riana sometimes had trouble keeping track of how long she'd been here. It felt like forever since she'd arrived. Like she'd known Cain—been fucking him—all her life.

But each morning when she woke up, she tried to tick off the days on her mental calendar. Today she thought she'd been in prison for a little over two months.

Cain had been here a lot longer.

This morning, as soon as the lights came on, he got up as usual and headed for the bathroom. But instead of washing up and starting his exercise routine, he crawled back into bed with her when he came out of the bathroom nook.

She rolled over on her side to peer at him. "You feeling all right?"

He had an odd look on his face, but he didn't look sick or upset. "Yeah."

"Horny?"

Occasionally, he jumped her as soon as they woke up, but he usually did so before the lights came back on.

Cain gave her a half smile and made a throaty humming noise that might have been an affirmation.

But he didn't roll over on top of her, and he didn't reach over to pull her close. He just lay on his back, one arm crossed beneath his head, and stared at the ceiling.

Genuinely confused by this change in his normal routine, she propped herself up on one elbow and stroked his chest with the other. His torso was solidly muscular, with rippling planes, coarse dark hair, and tight skin. "Cain? What's the matter?"

"Nothing." He turned his head slightly so he could gaze up at her, his eyes skimming appreciatively over her warm face and messy hair. Then they shifted down to her breasts, which were bare and exposed because she was holding herself up and the sheet had slipped down to her waist. She'd gone to sleep naked last night since she hadn't felt like putting her dirty clothes back on after she and Cain had fucked.

"You're acting weird," she told him, playing idly with one his nipples.

He gave a soft grunt. "I'm not sure, but I think today might be my birthday."

"Really?" She grinned down at him—although it was a silly thing to be excited about, given their circumstances. "How old are you?"

"Thirty-six today. If I've kept track of the days right since I got here."

She chuckled and stroked her hand up his chest to his neck. And then she caressed the stubbly skin of his jaw— enjoying the rough texture of it. "Getting kind of old, aren't you?"

He just smiled at her teasing. A real smile. The one she hardly ever saw.

Pleased with her success, she leaned down to press a soft kiss just next to his mouth. "Happy birthday," she murmured huskily. "Shall I give you a present?"

Cain gently pushed the hair back from her face as she mouthed a trail along his jaw. "What did you have in mind?"

She just made a purring sound and adjusted her body over him so she could kiss a line down his throat to his chest. She spent some time on his chest—flicking his nipples with her tongue and nibbling on a few spots she knew were sensitive.

His breathing picked up, and occasionally he would let out a textured sigh—sounds of pleasure that thrilled her and caused her pussy to clench in excitement.

Eventually, she scooted down his body even more until she was kissing his tight belly. She loved his abdomen and stroked it tenderly as she kissed slowly down toward his groin.

Soon her lips once again found coarse dark hair. And then she reached his cock, which was already halfway erect.

The covers had fallen off her completely and bunched up around her feet, so she posed her naked body as attractively as she could when she leaned down to lick a line along his cock.

He sucked in a sharp breath as she licked him, and his erection twitched visibly. She teased him for a few minutes—licking along the veins, fondling his balls, twirling her tongue around the head—until he was fully erect and the muscles of his thighs were tightly clenched.

Then she took his cock in her mouth and hollowed out her cheeks, sucking as well as she could.

Cain groaned softly and jerked his pelvis, making a little thrust up into her mouth.

Her pussy was wet now and starting to pulse. Riana closed one hand around the base of his cock and began a pattern of sucking and squeezing. She knew what Cain liked, so it wasn't hard to find the rhythm that made his body tighten and caused him to fist his hands in the bedding.

She shifted her eyes up to his face and saw his rigidly controlled expression. His eyes were hungry and possessive, though, as he lifted his head to watch her suck him.

He was doing his best to restrain his need to thrust, but occasionally his hips would give an erratic jerk. Riana didn't mind. She loved every sign that she was pleasing him. And so she worked his firm, warm flesh with her mouth as she breathed through her nose and bobbed her head.

When she reached down below her head to gently squeeze his balls, Cain gave a barely controlled thrust into her mouth. She slid her mouth back up his cock automatically, trying to avoid choking on his erection.

"Sorry," he gritted out, his skin glistening with perspiration as the muscles of his arms and belly rippled from holding himself rigidly in check.

She smiled around him and hummed an encouraging response. Then she held on to him firmly with one hand and took more of it in her mouth.

When she'd established her rhythm once more, she began to fondle his balls again. Her pussy was so wet now that she could feel the moisture leaking out, and she only got wetter as she saw how viscerally he responded to her ministrations.

She was completely focused on Cain, and so she barely registered the commentary that began from outside the bars of their cell. Vulgar comments, as usual, about her body, her position, and what she was doing to Cain.

She ignored them. By now, onlookers rarely fazed her, and what was more important was pleasing Cain.

But she sensed something change about his mood. And when she shifted her eyes up, she saw he was snarling slightly.

Afraid he was getting distracted and wouldn't enjoy the birthday blow job, she moved her free hand from his balls so she could rub little circles against the sensitive spot just behind his sac.

His whole body jerked, and he released a thick grunt.

She smiled again around his cock at her success.

Then she gasped in surprise when Cain leaned up, stretching his arms down on either side of her body. It took her several seconds to realize what he was doing.

He was pulling the covers back up over her, shielding her body from any oglers.

Riana fell out of rhythm for a minute, so surprised was she by his action. He'd never done anything like that before. He'd always ignored other prisoners who'd lurked at the bars—except for the first night when he'd told them to leave. She knew it was part of the power play. Acting like they bothered him—letting them bother him—only gave them power over him.

But now he'd made an obvious gesture. Hiding her from everyone else. Blocking their sight of how she was pleasuring him.

With the simple act, he'd made their coupling private. Somehow intimate in a very public place.

His eyes never left her face, never strayed from the sight of his shaft sliding in and out of her mouth. The sudden intimacy made Riana even more aroused, and she found herself unconsciously rocking her hips in a humping motion as she bobbed her head over him.

She massaged him with her fingers and sucked as hard as she could.

Cain clutched at the bedding beneath him as his face twisted.

Then he came. He groaned out a hoarse exclamation—one that sounded like it was ripped out of him—and his pelvis convulsed beneath her mouth. She could feel the spasms of his climax and prepared herself for his release, swallowing as much of it as she could.

Only a little dribbled out of the corner of her mouth as she gave his sated cock a few last, slow sucks.

Then she let it slide out of her lips as she hauled herself up and stretched out beside him, making sure to pull the covers up with her.

"Happy birthday," she murmured, kissing him leisurely on the lips, letting him taste himself there.

He smiled even as he kissed her, and his big hands slid down her back until they were cupping her ass. When their lips parted, he murmured, "Maybe my birthday is tomorrow."

She giggled appreciatively and rubbed herself against his body, feeling needy and incredibly turned on.

But it was his birthday, and the blow job had been a gift. She wasn't going to demand anything in return.

"That was incredible," he said, his voice deliciously deep and gravelly. "Thank you."

"You're welcome." Her clit was getting some good friction against his thigh, and she couldn't help but grind her pussy against it a little.

Before she could get anywhere in riding his thigh, he'd turned her over bodily. She was on her stomach now, and he was on top of her, his weight pushing her into the mattress.

She had no objections at all to this arrangement. In fact, she loved the feel of his hot, heavy body on top of her. But she squirmed beneath him and complained, "Hey, who told you to do that?"

Cain just chuckled, one of his hands squeezing under her body until he could rub her swollen clit. "You looked like you wanted a hump. I'll stop if you want me to."

"Don't you dare stop." She rocked her bottom to develop a good rhythm with her clit against his hand.

He rocked with her, his groin pressed into her ass and their bodies moving together under the covers. Riana gasped as the rhythm and the weight of his body mingled with the pressure of his fingers on her clit.

Soon the pressure at her center had deepened to such an extent that she writhed helplessly and made mewling sounds against the mattress.

She came, her hips riding out the pleasure between his pelvis and his hand.

He was starting to harden against her bottom already, so she kept pushing back against his groin.

After a minute, Cain grunted and lifted her by the hips so that her ass was higher than the rest of her. His legs on either side of hers, he parted her thighs enough to expose her slippery pussy.

Then he slid his newly hardened cock inside her.

Her chest and cheek still pressed down into the mattress, Riana gasped as Cain started to thrust, using the same rhythm they'd been mirroring before.

She whimpered as the erotic pressure kept rising inside her, and soon she buried her face in the bed so she could muffle her cries of pleasure.

Cain panted just beside her ear, supporting himself with his elbows and forearms, as he pushed into her in fast, hard thrusts.

Then Riana fell out of rhythm as the tension shattered inside her. She cried out into the mattress as the sensations sliced through her and her pussy contracted around Cain's cock.

He grunted in response. "Fuck, baby, so good."

Then his pelvis pistoned against her bottom, and he lost the rhythm too, groaning out another hard climax.

They collapsed together onto the bed in a tangle of hot, sweaty flesh.

Cain didn't roll off her immediately, and she didn't want him too either. She loved how it felt when he held on to her this way.

"That was a very good morning," Cain murmured at last, sounding hoarse and pleased and lazy.

"Yeah." Then Riana smiled to herself, thinking that sometimes just being with Cain brought a kind of light to her world that was totally absent here.

"What?" Cain demanded, pushing her hair out of her face so he could see a little more of it.

"I was just thinking," she admitted, knowing she couldn't tell him the truth of what she'd been feeling. "We should do it again tomorrow."

~

Other than their extended lovemaking first thing, the morning passed as nearly all their mornings did. On their midmorning run, however, something about Cain's demeanor struck her as different.

He usually ran with absolute focus, his eyes straight ahead as if he were channeling all his angst and energy into the motion of his body. But this morning, although he ran as hard as he ever did, he seemed watchful. And more than once she saw him studying various parts of the Hold.

It wasn't like he was on the hunt for an object to use for his device, but he had something on his mind—something other than exercise.

When she'd worn herself out, he locked her into their cell and took off at a run again. Breathless and bright red from her exertion, Riana splashed water on her face and then took off her sweat-soaked camisole, keeping her back to the bars of the cell so she didn't unnecessarily flash whomever might be passing by.

She'd done what she could to repair her outer shirt, but she mostly just wore her camisole now. It was on its last legs, and once it became too worn to wear, she wasn't sure what she would do.

Cain would find her something—she assumed. But she didn't like the idea of it.

When she'd washed up as best she could, she pulled on her button-up shirt so she could rinse out her top. She was gentle as she wrung the water out, wanting the fabric to last as long as possible.

When she left it to dry, she found her piece of a comb and started picking at her hair with it. She worked on it some every day and had basically gotten it to the point where it didn't feel so much like a rat's nest.

Hall was in his cell as normal. He hadn't come over to talk to her again after the last confrontation with Cain, but sometimes he would meet her eyes or smile.

She still wondered about him and sometimes wished she could talk to him more.

She ignored a random man who passed by the cell and started giving her a hard time about being a whore—one of Thorn's lackeys—but the man was still there when Cain returned from his run.

Cain calmly smashed his fist into the man's face before he unlocked and entered the cell.

Riana blinked in surprise. "That was unnecessarily violent. He wasn't doing anything unusual."

Cain's lip curled up in a snarl, but he didn't say anything as he walked over to the sink to clean up.

His softer, more tender mood from this morning had clearly vanished completely. He was back to being stoic and grumpy.

Riana wasn't surprised—Cain would never be a soft man—but she was a little disappointed. At times, she thought he was starting to open up to her more. That he was starting to think of her as a real companion, as a partner.

But she was continually reminded that he kept far more from her than he shared. He didn't treat her like a lover or even a friend—at least not all the time.

He was a very confusing man, and she wondered if he'd be so tight-lipped in different circumstances. Sometimes she wished she could get Hall to do her a favor and get a good read on what Cain was feeling about her.

She was pretty sure Cain liked her, cared for her at least to a certain extent. After that day a month ago when she'd almost been raped, she'd come to understand that much. He needed her. If not to survive, then at least to soften the stark, bleak lines of his life here.

But she wanted him to like her for real, to need her simply for who she was.

Not just because she was the only one he had.

As he washed up, she saw the old man she called the Tortoise doing his regular circuit of the Hold. He passed right outside the bars of the cell, and his eyes were focused downward. He looked somehow paler than normal, and she saw that his hands were shaking even more than they usually did. He swayed slightly midstep but evidently caught his balance and continued until he'd passed out of sight.

She felt a weird pang—something she hadn't experienced in a really long time.

"What is it?" Cain asked, turning around and seeing her preoccupation.

"That old man." She gestured toward where the man had disappeared. "The Tortoise. The one who goes around in circles."

He obviously knew whom she referred to. "What about him?"

"He looks like he's going to faint. I think he needs food." She wasn't sure why she'd even noticed it since she'd grown somewhat callous from the harshness of life here. But she felt that pang in her chest that spoke of concern, empathy. "Could you get him some food, do you think?"

Cain stared at her. "You want me to get him food?"

"I'm worried about him. He looks like he could drop dead."

"That might be a kindness."

She sucked in a breath. "You don't mean that. Maybe you could just give him my food then. I can stand to skip a meal, and he really needs it."

"What's gotten into you?" It was a real question. Cain's brows were drawn together, and he was watching her with obvious confusion on his face.

She sighed and leaned back against the wall. "I don't know. I know kindness is a sign of weakness here. I know if we're nice to one person, we'll be besieged on all sides." She closed her eyes. "I just don't always…"

"You don't always what?"

She opened her eyes to meet his. "I guess I don't want to really be what they've made us. Sorry. Never mind."

It had been a futile thought anyway. Nothing was going to change where they were, what they were, who they had become in this prison.

"I'll see what I can do."

She stiffened in surprise. "What?"

"At mealtime. Later. I'll see what I can do—without making a big deal."

The pang in her chest started to transform into something warm and full. "You will? For that poor man?"

Cain gave a strange, stiff nod. He didn't look soft in any way, but he felt almost vulnerable to her for just a moment. He muttered, "I don't want to be what they've made us either."

Then he went back to his device, kneeling on the floor to work on it.

She lay on the bed as she always did and watched, feeling like something had changed although she wasn't exactly sure what it was.

Cain worked for about an hour until Riana started getting drowsy. She was about to drift off to sleep when she noticed something odd about his manner.

He'd sat back on his heels and was just staring at the crude, ungainly machine. Sometimes he did that when he was trying to decide what kind of part he needed or when he was trying to work through how to design a certain section of it.

But he never sat back like this for so long, and he never had this particular expression on his face. He didn't look thoughtful or frustrated or impatient.

He looked watchful again—like he had earlier on his run. Quiet and almost wary.

Suddenly Riana wondered if he was done.

She turned her gaze to the device, but it didn't look significantly different from how it had before. He'd added a lot of new parts over the past two months, but they had all been small and hadn't made a significant difference in the appearance.

If it was done, though, why didn't he turn it on and test it out?

Maybe it couldn't perform its function in this cell. Maybe he didn't want any other prisoners to see what he'd made.

Or maybe he didn't want her to know he was done.

As if in response to that thought, Cain glanced back at where she was sprawled out. She gave him a groggy smile and half closed her eyes. This seemed to reassure him because he turned back to stare at his machine.

Her suspicions roused even further at this sign that he wanted to keep her unaware of whatever was going on here. Riana's gut churned, and her heart started to hammer.

He hadn't responded a month ago when she'd begged him not to leave her when he managed to escape. At the time, she hadn't been surprised or particularly worried. She hadn't really expected an answer to her plea.

But now she wondered if that should have been a warning.

He wouldn't leave her out of viciousness or cruelty, but maybe his escape plan would only work for one.

Maybe that was why he'd never let himself get truly close to her.

Because he'd always known he was going to have to leave her behind.

Cain stared at the machine for a long time while Riana pretended to doze.

But she was brutally on edge and, even though her eyes were closed, she knew when he stood up.

She could sense him looking at her for a several seconds, and she wondered if he knew she wasn't asleep. He didn't say anything though, and soon she heard him moving in the cell. She heard a scraping sound and knew exactly what it was.

He was moving the device.

That did it. She jumped up from the bed, unconsciously smoothing out her disarranged shirt. "Going on the hunt?" she asked cheerily when Cain's head jerked up to stare at her.

He'd moved the machine over toward the door of the cell.

Swallowing over the lump of fear in her throat, she continued, "I'll come too."

Cain shook his head, a tight, unreadable expression on his face. "No. Why don't you stay here this afternoon?"

Riana's hands fisted at her sides. "I don't want to stay here. I always go with you. Why can't I go today?"

"I've got something to do. You can't come." He turned his back on her as if his words had settled the question.

A wave of terror and rage slammed into Riana, and she acted on instinct and panic rather than any sane reason or sense. She strode over and grabbed him by the arm, holding on as hard as she could. "I'm going to come. I'm not going to stay here!"

Cain turned back around and stared at her, but he didn't look as astonished by her intensity as torn. He pulled his arm away from her grip and reached out to hold her by the upper arms. "You have to stay. There's no argument here."

His tone was even and filled with absolute authority.

All of it was only assuring Riana that he was about to leave her. That he was going to make his escape. Without her.

She struggled in his grip, trying to pull away so she could hit him, pound on his chest, somehow express the panic, rage, and betrayal she was feeling.

"Riana," Cain gritted out, his hands like iron, utterly unbreakable. "Stop it. What's gotten into you?"

"Don't do it," she choked, the one thread of her mind that could still think rationally telling her to keep her voice down so no one else could hear. "Don't leave me, Cain. You know I'll die here without you. You can't just leave me behind!"

Something tightened on his stoic face. "What?"

"I know you're done. I'm not stupid. I know you're taking it to do whatever it does." She nodded helplessly down at the device. She was practically sobbing now but without tears. She was far too horrified to cry. "And now you're leaving without me. After everything, how can you—"

"Riana!" The one word was as sharp as the bite of a blade. He shook her a little to get her attention.

She fell silent, his face blurring in front of her eyes.

"What the fuck is wrong with you?" He sounded furious. Impatient. Almost disgusted. And for some reason the very human tone from him comforted her. "I'm not going to leave you behind."

Her mouth dropped open, and she stared at him, too dazed to take it all in.

If possible, Cain looked even angrier. "Stop looking like you can't believe it. What the fuck kind of monster do you think I am? I'm not going to leave you here."

"You're not?" She sounded like an idiot—even to her own ears.

"Of course not." He shook her a little more although not nearly hard enough to hurt. "Of course you're coming too."

The knot of panic was finally relaxing inside her— leaving an overwhelming flood of warmth and relief. "Oh."

Still looking annoyed with her, Cain explained in a low voice, "I am finished with it. I think it will work if I can figure out a plan to use it to our advantage. I need to find a place to put this thing so it can… do its job."

Riana frowned as her hazy mind tried to keep up. "But—"

"Unfortunately, it's not a spaceship to fly us out of here." His voice was dry and sharp now, and she understood why. Obviously it wasn't a spaceship. The jumbled parts barely looked like a working machine. "I've got a couple of ideas, but I need to scout them out and it's too distracting if you're with me since I'm always worrying about keeping you safe."

"Oh." She squirmed with sudden embarrassment. "I thought you were moving the thing now and then going to leave me."

"I'll have to wait until lights out to move it. I was just seeing how heavy it was. But first I've got to find the best place to put it if you'll let me leave for a minute."

"Oh. Sorry. I guess I was stupid."

His eyes narrowed. "Yeah."

"Well, you don't need to be snotty. I was scared, and you're always going around keeping secrets. I didn't know."

Something colder than impatience flickered in his eyes. "You should have known. Unless you genuinely think I am a monster."

"I don't," she admitted, reaching out to touch his chest, worried she'd actually hurt him and that was what triggered his coldness. "But we're all on survival instincts here. And if your escape plan could only handle one..." Her voice trailed off as she remembered her intense terror of losing him.

His face softened unexpectedly, and he stroked her cheek with his knuckle. "I see. I don't have it all completely worked out yet, but whatever the plan ends up being, it will have to work for two."

Riana managed a shaky smile at him. "Good." They held the look for several seconds, and it felt like they shared something in the gaze.

Then Riana glanced down at his precious device. "What does that thing even do?"

"I have no guarantee it will do anything. I'll explain when I get back."

She wanted to know right now, but she just nodded and stepped back, recognizing that this was important and she couldn't get in his way.

He locked the door behind him and disappeared out of sight.

Several minutes later, she heard an uproar. Maybe a fight. Maybe something else. She couldn't really tell by the nature of the noise. She assumed it was Cain's doing. In a few seconds he appeared at the door of the cell again. Before she could open her mouth to ask what was going on, he'd picked up the device and left again.

He must have shaped some sort of distraction so he could plant it—so he wouldn't have to wait until after lights out and fumble around in the dark.

She huddled on the bed, trying not to get scared until Cain reappeared. She was so glad to see him she jumped off the bed and threw herself into his arms.

She'd never done anything like that before, but she wasn't even self-conscious. Cain felt a little stiff at first—maybe from surprise—but then he put his arms around her and held her close for a minute.

"Did you not believe me when I said I'd be back?" Cain muttered eventually.

She pulled her face away from his shoulder. "I did. But I'm all confused and nervous, and now you've given me hope that maybe we can actually get out of here. I'm so edgy I can barely stand it."

"I know," Cain murmured, stroking her back with a surprisingly gentle hand. "I've been putting this plan together for a year now, and I'm still not sure of the final details. I have to think things through myself before I share them. I wasn't holding out on you on purpose. I didn't realize you'd catch me at it, put together an absurd theory, and go into a panic about it."

To Riana's surprise, she realized he was actually apologizing to her for keeping her in the dark for so long. She felt a warmth fill her chest and squirmed a little in pleasure. But keeping her voice dry, she muttered, "It was a perfectly reasonable theory."

Cain actually chuckled.

"Can't you please tell me what's going on now?" Riana begged, fisting her fingers in his shirt. "I feel like I'm going to go crazy."

"Yeah. I'll try to explain what I've got in place so far, but I'm still not sure of the final details."

"Well, maybe I can help with those. I do have a brain that basically functions, you know."

Cain sat down on the edge of the bed, pulled her down to sit down next to him, and started to explain.

Several minutes later, Riana was staring at him, thinking as quickly as she could. His plan wasn't bad—it could possibly work—but it required them getting into the control room, which was going to be a really hard thing to manage.

After a minute, her mind landed on the obvious answer.

"Hall," she whispered. "We can get Hall to help."

Cain stiffened. "I don't think so."

"Well, why not? If we can get to a transport, there's room for three people as well as two. And Hall has that Reader power that might be exactly what we need."

"I'm not going to trust both of our lives to him. We have no reason to think he's on our side."

She was getting frustrated since Cain seemed to be acting on testosterone rather than reason. "Well, we can trust that he wants to get out of here as much as we do. What is he going to do? Ruin the only chance he has to escape by tattling?"

"He could turn me in and take what I know he wants." Cain's expression was completely impenetrable.

"What is that?"

"You. And this cell."

She groaned. "Cain, please. If he has a choice between escape and this cell, which do you think he's going to take? He's a smart guy, and he has a certain ability that we might need. Is it even possible that I might have an idea that contributes to our getting out of here, or am I really just a possession to you?"

She hadn't intended to ask the final question, but it burst out before she could stop it.

It lingered in the air, defined the space between them.

Cain breathed heavily, but he didn't argue anymore. He was obviously thinking, weighing options until finally he relaxed slightly and nodded. "Okay. But we don't tell him until tomorrow. I don't want him to have any chance to come up with his own alternate plan."

"Agreed." Her chest had loosened, and for the first time in so long she felt something like hope.

It definitely had to do with the slim possibility of their escaping, but it also had to do with the fact that Cain had given weight to her opinion, treated her like an equal partner.

She wondered what he was thinking about the future, whether there was any chance that he'd want them to stay together.

She wondered if this crazy plan—even Cain's ungainly machine—would even work.

After they'd talked, they had sex—slow, quiet missionary under the covers. Riana was drained and clingy after her stressful day and her scare. And after his two climaxes that morning, Cain was able to take his time without urgency taking over.

The motion seemed to match the deep emotion she was feeling. Riana kept her arms around his back, holding him as tightly as she wanted. And Cain thrust into her with a slow, steady rhythm, angling his hips to give her as much pleasure as he could.

She'd come a second time when the noise outside the cell altered. It wasn't the mealtime roar. And it wasn't the sudden burst of sound that followed the outbreak of a violent altercation.

She wasn't quite sure what it was.

Cain was getting close to coming. His speed had picked up, and his expression was tightening. But he must have noticed her distraction because he gritted out, "Checkup."

That was it. The armored vehicle must have entered the Hold to pick up the next prisoner for a checkup.

Riana moved her hands up so she could stroke his scalp, loving the texture of his closely shaven hair beneath her fingertips. "Are you going to come?"

"Was thinking about it." His hips jerked a few times as if he momentarily lost control of them.

She squeezed her pussy around his cock. "Oh good."

He grunted at the pressure, and his features twisted with effort.

She squeezed him again.

He let out a muffled exclamation, and a wash of pleasure transformed his face as he pushed a few last times into her tight pussy.

She pulled him down into her arms afterward, feeling oddly tender and possessive. He breathed heavily against the crook of her neck, and then he pulled up to look down at her face.

She thought he was going to say something, but he didn't have the chance.

The noise of the armored vehicle had been getting closer and closer.

Until it suddenly appeared just in front of the cell.

It stopped there, and both Riana and Cain turned to stare at it in surprise.

It only took her a second to figure out what was happening. One of them was getting taken for the checkup.

The thought nauseated her even though she had no idea what the checkup consisted of, and she was suddenly terrified that the timing was intentional. That somehow their plan or his device had been discovered.

"Just a coincidence," Cain murmured under his breath, obviously having read her silent terror. "Don't panic."

There was a mechanized claw at the front of the vehicle, which was usually the way they picked up the prisoners for the checkup—so the guard could avoid leaving the protection of the vehicle and risking attack. But since there were bars in front of this cell, the claw couldn't do its duty. So instead the guard pulled the vehicle alongside the bars until the door to the vehicle was lined up with the door to the cell.

Pretty clever, actually. That way, there was no risk of being attacked by the other prisoners.

Not that Cain himself wasn't threat enough.

When the door opened, Riana understood she wasn't the only one who realized this. The first thing she saw was a gun—an old-fashioned automatic weapon which was all they used in the Hold, probably as a precaution against one of the prisoners getting ahold of a more sophisticated weapon. Then she saw Davis lean out. "Unlock the cell," he called out.

Neither Cain nor Riana moved. They were still entangled intimately under the covers, and they just stared at the unexpected arrival.

"I have no qualms about killing one or both of you." Davis didn't sound vicious or nasty. Simply matter-of-fact.

With a long exhalation, Cain extracted himself from Riana's arms and sat on the edge of the bed to pull on his pants. Then he walked over to unlock the cell door.

Davis wasn't stupid. He leaned back as Cain approached, making sure the gun was out of the range of Cain's hands.

But Cain didn't put up a fight. She hadn't expected him to.

Escape was almost within reach. He wasn't going to blow it now.

Evidently, it was Cain's turn for a checkup because he was manacled at his wrists and feet. And then, to her horror, he was gagged.

"Why are you doing that?" Riana gasped, sitting up and barely remembering to pull up the sheet to hide her bare breasts.

"Protocol," Davis explained calmly. "When we can't use the claw."

"Oh."

Only when he was being hauled over to the entrance of the vehicle did Cain begin to struggle. He was trying to say something around his gag, and he jerked and fought against his restraints.

Davis aimed a hard blow at his side, causing Cain to briefly double over.

"No," Riana cried out. "Don't." She was so upset she started out of the bed, forgetting the fact that she was naked and that Cain's semen was leaking out of her pussy.

Davis turned back to her. She saw his eyes slide down to take in the sight of her body, and a new expression appeared on his face.

It only lasted a moment, however, before he regained his businesslike passivity.

But the brief flare of heat she'd seen made her self-conscious, and she pulled one of the blankets off the bed and held it up to shield her body.

By that point she'd figured out what Cain was trying to express. So she explained, "The key. To this cell. There's only one of them, and he has it. I think he wants to give it to me." Her eyes strayed to the rest of the Hold. "Otherwise, I'll have no protection here."

Davis thought for a minute but then must have decided this was reasonable. He went over to Cain himself and took the key. After studying it for a minute to make sure that was all it was, he walked it back over to Riana.

His eyes held hers for a long moment. "Are you all right here?"

It was an absolutely idiotic question. No one could be all right in the Hold.

But she understood what he was asking her. His eyes had drifted over to Cain's big, animalistic form.

"As well as can be expected." She kept her eyes cool even though she suspected Davis was being as kind as he was allowed to be.

He'd kept her from being raped by the other guards that first day. She remembered that.

With a curt nod, Davis turned away from her and herded a shackled Cain onto the vehicle. Riana felt vaguely sick as the doors of the vehicle slammed shut, but she hurried over to lock the door of the cell before it pulled away.

Davis wouldn't torture Cain for fun, and he wouldn't kill him unless Cain put up a fight.

It should be all right.

It was terrible that the checkup happened just before they were going to make their escape, but it wasn't the end of the world.

Cain would be back before lights out.

She spent the rest of the day huddled in bed. She wasn't about to leave the cell at mealtime to try to get any food, but she wasn't hungry anyway.

If Cain had been here, he would have found the Tortoise and given him something to eat.

Hall came over, standing outside the bars until Riana noticed him and sat up.

"Do you need anything?" Hall asked the way he had last time. This time he added, "I can get you some food."

She shook her head. "I'm not hungry. But thanks."

"Are you going to be all right in here by yourself?"

"He'll be back before lights out."

"Are you sure?"

Her breath hitched because it was a fear she had herself. "Of course. It's a checkup. He'll be back."

Hall inclined his head although he didn't look convinced.

"He'll be back," Riana repeated as if saying it enough would make it true.

"Chances are, he will," Hall said. "If the worst happens, and he doesn't come back, I can help you. You'll need someone."

She nodded jerkily, knowing he was right, knowing that if anything happened to Cain, Hall would be her best and only option. He might not be as strong as Cain, but he seemed to do all right. He still had his cell, and everyone else seemed to avoid him because of his gift. He wouldn't hurt her.

The thought of fucking him made her feel faintly sick—not because he was unattractive or because she doubted his virility, but because he wasn't Cain.

And the only way she'd be in the position to fuck anyone else was if Cain were dead.

"I watch you sometimes," Hall said in a different, almost reflective tone.

She stiffened. "You aren't the only one."

Hall made a face. "If I wanted to see fucking, I could see that anywhere. That's not why I watch you."

She was confused now and genuinely curious. There seemed to be depths to Hall she hadn't even scratched the surface of, and she doubted she ever would. "So why do you then?"

"Because it's too easy to forget in this place what it means to be human. And I can see it still in you." He nodded toward the corner of the cell where Cain's device had been. "And even him. It's kept me sane."

Riana was strangely touched by the admission, by its obvious sincerity—so unlike the ironic charisma that seemed to be his typical demeanor. "Thanks," she mumbled, not sure what else to say.

He'd turned away to leave, obviously seeing the conversation was over, when she called out after him, "Hall."

He looked back with a lift of his eyebrows.

"Tomorrow. We could use your help tomorrow."

She saw his face change as he processed the words, knew he'd understood what she was saying. He glanced over yet again to the floor of the cell where the device used to be.

"I'll be here. Say the word."

"We'll let you know."

"Thank you," he said just before he walked away. "If I have to stay here much longer, I'm going to kill myself."

The words were light, almost carefree, but Riana suspected they were true.

The rest of the day seemed to drag on unmercifully, and her reasonable calm at Cain's departure gradually altered into anxious dread.

What was happening to him? What were they doing? Were they hurting him? When was she going to get him back?

She couldn't keep track of time in her mind as well as Cain did, so she could never predict the exact time of lights out the way he did. She was sure it was getting close though.

They were going to give him back to her this evening, weren't they?

She was starting to have nightmares about them keeping Cain overnight when a voice outside of the cell startled her.

"Riana. Let me in!"

She jumped out of bed at the sound of Cain's voice, and she stumbled over to unlock the door.

Only when she'd let him in did she have a chance to look him over.

He looked terrible. There wasn't any evident damage to his body, but he was limping and hunched over. His face looked stretched and exhausted.

She grabbed him and hugged him to her. "Cain, are you all right?"

"Yeah." His low mutter wasn't convincing, and he pulled out of her embrace.

"What did they do to you?"

He didn't answer. Just gave a brief shake of his head and limped into the bathroom. When he came out, he washed his hands and face in the sink and stood blankly in the middle of the floor.

"Cain, tell me what's wrong," she begged, feeling helpless and scared and overwhelmed.

He rubbed at his face. "I'm all right." This time he seemed to be making the effort to sound convincing.

But Riana still wasn't convinced.

Instead of demanding answers, her eyes overflowed with sympathy. She put an arm around him and urged him toward the bed.

He didn't resist. When he'd gotten into bed, he rolled onto his side, facing away from her. He seemed to be closing in on himself.

She made a choked sound in her throat and pressed her body up against his back, wrapping her arms around him. She stroked his chest, hating how tense and stiff his muscles felt.

He'd gone fully into defense mode, and she had no idea what they'd done to him to make him.

Pressing kisses on his shoulder and the back of his neck, she murmured silly, soothing words and stroked and caressed him as much as she could. The lights went off, leaving them in darkness, but she didn't stop touching him.

It wasn't remotely sexual, and it wasn't going to turn into that. But the feeling in her gut and her chest—deep, swelling, overwhelming—was every bit as strong as physical arousal. She felt tender, protective, almost maternal. She wanted to take care of him. Wanted to make him feel better.

And had no idea how she could do it.

So she kept stroking and kissing him softly until his body started to relax at last. His breathing slowed down, became thick and hoarse. And finally he turned around in her arms so he could hold her as tightly as she was holding him.

Intensely relieved at these signs that he was recovering, Riana snuggled up against his chest. Eventually she whispered into the dark, "Can you tell me what they did to you?"

One of Cain's hands was tangled in her hair, holding her head against his shoulder. His other hand, stroking her lower back, stilled as he replied, "Not now. I'll try to tell you tomorrow."

She didn't push him any further. She knew he meant what he'd said. He wanted to tell her, but he wasn't psychologically able to open up to that extent yet—not after his defenses were just starting to come down.

"All right," she murmured, pressing another kiss against his skin, tasting the salty bite of him. He even smelled different—like whatever they'd done had affected the raw, natural scent of him. She hated the change and wanted him to smell like himself again. "Just go to sleep now. We'll worry about everything else tomorrow."

FIVE

Riana woke the following morning feeling like something was different. After over two months of endless days—all exactly the same—the feeling was significant enough to jar her awake from her usual half-conscious daze.

Cain wasn't going to leave her. He was going to take her with him when he tried to escape. They'd worked out a plan. It was a long shot, but it was possible. Hall might not be wholly trustworthy, but he wanted to get out of here as much as they did, so they could trust him in this, at least. There might be hope for life outside the Hold—when she'd spent weeks telling herself not to even dream of a miracle rescue.

It wasn't a miracle though. It was just Cain being Cain. And evidence that she meant something to him—at least enough to trust her judgment and to not leave her behind.

She shifted in bed and realized she was snuggled up next to him. She had somehow scooted down while she'd slept because her cheek was pressed up against the side of Cain's belly.

It wasn't the worst place to be.

She pulled away, the skin of her cheek clinging to Cain's warm, hard flesh as they parted. When she glanced up, she saw that he was already awake.

He didn't look damaged or defensive the way he had the night before. His expression was unfamiliar though—quiet and almost reflective.

"Hi," she said, her voice cracking on the word.

With a faint smile, he murmured huskily, "What are you doing down there?"

Riana scooted back up so that she was stretched along his side. "I don't know." One of her cheeks felt warmer than the other so she assumed one was bright red from being pressed up against his side for so long.

He adjusted so that he could wrap his arms around her. He inhaled deeply as if he were breathing her in—which was a little unnerving since she was quite sure she didn't smell very good.

"Are you all right?" she asked, peering up at his unreadable expression. Her heart still ached at how he'd been feeling the night before.

"I'm all right. Thanks." This morning his words rang true.

She opened her mouth to ask about what had happened at the checkup, but then she snapped it shut again. She didn't want to pressure him or make him think about it this morning when he was clearly feeling better.

But he must have read her mind. Because after clearing his throat, he began, "It's not torture."

Riana gasped, startled and relieved at the same time. She didn't bother asking for clarification since she knew exactly what he was referring to. "It's not?"

"No." He shook his head slowly and brushed his hand along the tangles in her hair. "Davis is rigid about following Coalition rules. So the checkups get done once a year, and they are legitimate checkups."

"So what's so terrible about it?"

Cain was obviously having a hard time saying it even though he sustained a low, even tone the whole time. "They strap you down to a table naked to do a visual examination, and then you're moved along on a conveyor belt through a series of machines to scan and test your health."

She could only imagine how Cain would feel bound and humiliated that way. She could only imagine how she herself would feel. But there must be more to it than that, based on his behavior last night. "Do the tests hurt?"

"Some of them. But the worst thing is…" He trailed off, wincing slightly.

"What?" She stroked his chest and belly and felt woozy—so powerfully did she sympathize with Cain's obvious distress. "What is it?"

"You move through a tube—so small and tight you couldn't move even if you weren't strapped down. And the tests take hours."

Hours. Trapped in a tiny, dark enclosure. And Cain didn't like to be boxed in. He'd told her so the first night she'd met him.

She understood his reaction. Another person might not have responded so intensely, but he had. He wasn't invulnerable. So she didn't ask any more questions. She just squeezed him in a hug and rested her head on his shoulder.

After a minute, Cain said, "But ultimately, I think this might help us."

Riana lifted her head. "How?"

"I had an idea while I was there. There might now be an easier way to get into the control room."

"What way?"

Cain met her eyes evenly, something oddly wary in his eyes. "Today Davis will take you up for a checkup."

"What? Wait a minute! What? How do you know?"

"I know." When he saw she was about to object and demand further information, he explained, "He's got a thing for you. And now you're on his mind. He's not going to want to wait to bring you up."

She was so startled she sat up in bed and gaped at him. "What are you talking about? He doesn't have a thing for me. He barely even acknowledges me—or any other prisoner, for that matter." But she remembered the hot look she'd caught in Davis's eyes the day before when she'd gotten out of the bed naked. She started to wonder if Cain might be right.

"He's a professional, but he definitely has a thing for you. I noticed it the first day he showed you around."

"He's never even tried to—"

"He wouldn't. He wouldn't rape a prisoner even though it would be so easy. But he's interested. I talked you up while I was up there."

"What?" Her startled question came out louder than she'd expected.

"It's not what you think. I didn't make it sound like I was pimping you out—he'd never be convinced by that. I made a lot of crude remarks about you to him so his heroic side would get riled up. I'm positive he'll come get you for a checkup this afternoon. And we can take advantage of it."

Riana was starting to follow his line of thought—although she was still disturbed by the idea of Davis's possible interest. And she started to see possibilities in such a straightforward way of getting out of the prison hold and into a better position to escape.

Maybe they could get out of here after all.

Maybe they could get out of here today.

She saw across the distance, through the bars, that Hall was looking in their direction. She glanced over at Cain.

He nodded. "Get him over here. We're going to need him."

~

"Tell me what you can do," Cain demanded curtly but not angrily.

Hall had been listening to the plan they'd put together with impressive calm and efficiency—as if escaping from inescapable prison planets was something he did every day.

"I can sense what someone is feeling, and I can turn it around on them," Hall explained. His eyes shifted from Riana to Cain. "For instance, when you were punching me before, you were feeling rage and violence, so I turned it around on you—making you feel the opposite. So you'd stop."

"So you can manipulate people into feeling the opposite of what they're really feeling?" Riana asked.

"Pretty much."

"So if someone is feeling wary and careful…," Cain began.

"If I touch them, I can make them not care at all."

"How long can you hold it?" Cain asked.

"In a weak-willed person, I can hold it for upward of an hour. But not everyone. I'd say we can't rely on more than five minutes."

"That will be enough." Cain looked over at Riana. "And you're going to be okay stalling for a while? It will take some time for us to get into place."

"I can stall." She sounded more confident than she felt, but she was willing to do whatever she needed to do.

She'd been forced into helplessness for the past two months, and it was almost a relief to finally be able to something—however dangerous—that was genuinely a proactive step.

The three of them looked at each other for a minute, and there was a silent, mutual understanding between them.

"All right then," Cain said. "We better be ready."

"And your ramshackle device is really going to work?" Hall asked, looking amused and faintly smug, more like his old self than she'd seen him in a long time.

Cain glowered. "It will work. Just make sure your thing works."

Hall was opening his mouth to reply when Riana interrupted with a throaty exclamation of impatience. "Damn it. Would you guys stop with the male showdown? You might as well be arguing about penis size."

Hall laughed out loud, and after a few moments, Cain gave her a look that felt warm, special. She wished she weren't so nervous so she could enjoy it.

She should have known by now not to doubt Cain.

He wasn't the brute, mindless predator he appeared on first sight. That morning, he'd made a point of finding the Tortoise and giving him food, in spite of his narrow focus on their escape. He was far more intelligent and articulate than he appeared. And he was clearly a strategist—gifted at reading people, situations, and undercurrents and making plans accordingly.

He was nearly always right.

Davis did come for her that afternoon to take her to the checkup.

Cain had been doing one-arm push-ups—working off some of his excess energy—and Riana had just been lying on the bed, trying to distract herself from her anxiety by admiring the sleek power of his rippling muscles and the primal masculinity of his body, covered with the sheen of perspiration.

When the vehicle pulled up beside the cell, just as it had the day before, Riana got up immediately and stood by the bed.

"Unlock the cell," Davis called out.

Cain pulled himself up from the floor and stood stock still, glaring in the direction of the vehicle. He looked grim, stubborn, bristling, and he made no move to follow the curt order.

"Do it." Davis aimed a gun at him.

Riana hurried over to Cain and grabbed the key from his pocket. Then she went to unlock the cell door as instructed.

Davis came in, warily leveling the weapon at Cain.

"You took me yesterday," Cain snarled.

"I'm not here for you today." Davis's eyes flickered over to where Riana was standing a few feet away.

Cain made a growling noise and took a threatening step forward.

Davis shifted the gun until he was aiming directly at Cain's groin. "Not a good idea. I'm just taking her for the checkup. She'll be back before lights out."

"She's mine," Cain gritted out, looking and sounding like a snarling animal.

"Don't be ridiculous," Riana snapped, stepping between Cain and Davis's weapon with an impatient glance back at Cain.

"I'll go," she said, calmly meeting Davis's eyes. "And I'm not his."

As she'd hoped, his expression changed as she added those last soft words. He nodded, an expression of both understanding and interest on his face.

He'd also turned his body some so he was facing in their direction, leaving his back toward the toilet nook.

Without making a sound, Hall stepped out of the nook where he'd been hiding for hours, and put his hand out to grip the back of Davis's neck.

Davis lowered his gun, and his face became strangely, frighteningly blank.

Cain took the gun out of his hands—facing no resistance at all—and then he ducked into the vehicle to make sure there was no other guard inside. Evidently, there wasn't. Davis had come on his own yesterday too.

It was tempting to think they could all just get into the vehicle and make their way out of the prison and then to a transport that would get them off the planet. But far too many guards would be waiting when the vehicle returned, and they'd never get access to the control room or get through to the docking station.

"Is he ready?" Cain asked, his eyes on Hall.

Hall nodded. "He was highly on guard, so now he's not. But hurry." His face had broken out in perspiration, and Riana realized it must take effort to hold the Reader's connection the way he was.

Cain asked, "Is there a transport we could use to get off the planet?"

Davis nodded, that same blank, apathetic expression on his face. "In Docking Bay D."

Riana took a shaky breath.

"How do we get through the locked doors in this place?"

"Bracelet." Davis waved his hand around, and she saw a metal bracelet around his wrist with a few different blinking lights.

She was relieved the doors didn't activate by an eye scan. Maybe it was another safety precaution—so guards wouldn't go around losing their eyes. She reached for the bracelet, trying to get it off, but it wouldn't budge.

"Can you take it off?" she asked, feeling desperate since Hall's face was getting more and more strained.

"Sure." Davis clicked something on the bracelet, and it snapped apart.

She took it from him, fumbling slightly in her nerves. "He'll notice it's gone," she murmured to Cain.

He nodded, studying the bracelet, evidently to figure out what made it work.

"Hurry," Hall muttered, shifting from foot to foot. "This guy's will is not weak." The arm he had raised to hold against Davis's neck was shaking visibly.

Cain exhaled audibly as he snapped a piece out of the bracelet. Then he snapped the rest of the bracelet back on Davis's wrist. He pocketed the piece he'd taken out. "That's the part that matters," he told her. "The rest is just to hold it on the wrist."

She really hoped he was right.

"Okay," Cain said. "Get him back in the vehicle."

Hall was already moving, pushing Davis with him. "He'll be susceptible for a minute after I let him go. Give him a story to believe. Make it a good one.

Cain was putting the manacles and gag on Riana although he left the gag hanging rather than tightening it, and then he helped her into the vehicle. She felt sick and helpless and terrified, but she forced the feelings down because now was the moment that really mattered.

Cain leaned down and murmured into her ear. "I'll be coming for you. No matter what. Wait for me."

She nodded mutely, a painful tension in her throat, and then she watched as Cain deboarded the vehicle and then met Hall's eyes.

"Get in position," Hall said hoarsely, clearly on his last thread of control. "I have to move quick."

Then Cain was out of sight, and Hall was saying, "Now."

Hall was off the vehicle, shutting the door behind him before she could process his exit.

Davis was standing in the armored vehicle, swaying and sickeningly white.

"Are you okay?" she asked, not having to fake the anxiety in her voice. "Are you okay?"

He blinked in her direction. "What... happened?"

"I don't know. You were putting the gag on me, and then it was like you blacked out or something. Do you feel okay?"

"No." He lowered himself to one of the seats, breathing slowly. "We were leaving?"

"Yeah. He was getting out of control, so you had to knock him out, and then you were getting me ready to take for checkup." She had no idea how Hall's ability worked, but she prayed desperately that Davis would believe the story.

Still looking dazed, Davis glanced out the window of the vehicle to see Cain lying on the floor of the cell, evidently unconscious. Hall was nowhere in sight.

Davis's face was clearing and gaining more color, and he looked a little less dizzy as he said, "I don't know what happened. Everything just faded. It's never happened to me before."

"Maybe you should see a doctor." She kept her face relaxed and her eyes wide. "There are some medical conditions that cause that. Hopefully it's nothing too serious."

"Yes." He must have pulled himself together because he reached over to the gag hanging lose under her chin.

"Do you have to put that on?" she asked, her pulse starting to race again.

"It's protocol. It won't be for long."

She nodded, unable to say anything since he was strapping the gag in place. Then he went to sit in front of the controls of the vehicle and steered it to the entrance of the prison.

She had a brief moment of panic, thinking he wouldn't have the thing in his bracelet that triggered the doors, but they opened automatically, evidently controlled by one of the guards on the other side.

When they docked next to the control center of the prison, a few guards came out—all of them brandishing guns. Davis helped her out of the vehicle, looking like himself again.

The story she'd planted had evidently been believable.

She noticed one of the guards eyeing her greedily, his gaze crawling over her body. Her trousers had been so well-worn by now that the fabric was soft and thin, riding low on her hips and smoothly shaping the lines of her bottom and legs. She was just wearing her camisole. The thin straps were stretched so they always fell down over her shoulders, and the worn fabric clung, revealing the swell of her breasts and the peaks of her nipples and leaving a strip of bare skin between the hem and the top of her pants.

She was in better shape than she'd ever been in her life—thanks to two months of rigorous exercise with Cain. But she also hadn't taken a shower in two months. And she couldn't believe anyone but Cain would actually find her attractive.

"I'll take over the checkup if you want," the guard volunteered.

Davis looked briefly annoyed, but then his professional demeanor reappeared as he snapped out an order to the others about preparing for mealtime.

So it was Davis who walked Riana through a different mechanized door, and it was Davis who took the gag off her.

After clearing her throat, Riana asked weakly, "What are you going to do to me?"

"Checkup. There's nothing to be afraid of."

Again Riana realized his words were a gesture of kindness—although they didn't feel particularly kind to her at the moment. She knew what was coming, and she would have been afraid—if she'd believed she would actually be going through with the checkup.

"Isn't there a... a doctor?"

"We have no doctor here. The machines do most of the work anyway. You need to take off your clothes and lie down here." Davis gestured at the long table in the center of the room. "Put your arms and legs on the cuffs, and I'll snap them in place from outside."

Even though she'd known it was coming, the words still made her belly churn with nerves. "Do I have to take my clothes off?" she asked since she knew she'd need to stall until Cain and Hall got into place. "Those other guards were—"

"No one will see you but me," Davis assured her. "Unless you don't get on the table to be restrained. Then I'll have to bring others in, and we'll do it by force."

"I'll do what I'm supposed to." She spoke quickly and widened her eyes, not having to feign anxiety. "I don't want any trouble."

This seemed to please Davis too. The corner of his lips turned up slightly. "I didn't think so. I'll be outside, but I'll have to observe you through the window to make sure you don't try anything."

"I understand."

When Davis had left the room, the door sliding shut behind him, Riana took off her clothes, draping them on an empty table. She felt trembly and uncomfortable, completely naked—especially knowing Davis was watching her—but she got on the table, laid on her back, and put her heels and hands in the designated spots.

There was a loud click as the shackles snapped over her wrists and ankles. She was naked on the table now, spread-eagle with her legs parted.

The only time she could remember feeling more vulnerable was when she'd first been dumped into the Hold.

Davis wasn't going to hurt her though. He might not be a truly good man, but he was a rule follower, and he wasn't out to hurt or debase her.

She would have come to this conclusion on her own, but she was comforted by the fact that Cain had assessed the man in the same way.

Cain wouldn't have let her do this if he hadn't been confident she was safe with Davis.

"Are you cold?" Davis asked when he came back into the room.

She was. Her skin had broken out in goose bumps, and her nipples had tightened into erect peaks. "A little." Her voice came out shaky, so she didn't have to try to pretend. "The table is really cold."

Davis hadn't looked at her directly yet—as if he were making a point not to—and now he turned to adjust one of the controls on the panel that covered half of one wall. "I'll see if we can get it a little warmer in here."

Riana whispered, "Thank you."

He met her eyes then, still managing to avoid staring down at her spread, naked body. "I'll give you a visual checkup first—to look for obvious signs of ill health. Then you'll go through a series of computerized tests. It's uncomfortable, but you should do fine."

"Okay." She really, really hoped Cain was getting things in motion soon.

She assumed he would be okay until he'd triggered the machine. Then all hell would break loose, and they'd all be in a lot of danger.

For the first time, Davis let his eyes stray down to her body. They lingered on her firm, rounded breasts although he clearly tried not to leer. "Has anything been troubling you?"

Other than the fact that she'd been thrown in a prison to be used as the convicts wanted—she assumed he meant.

"My skin is itchy a lot because I can't clean myself properly," she told him although she assumed this would be true of everyone. "And I have a couple of cuts I'm afraid are infected."

Davis had looked over her body carefully, doing his best to sustain a professional disinterest. But she'd noticed his breathing pick up and his face flush slightly, and she was pretty sure they were signs of excitement. "Where are the cuts?"

"One is here." She gestured with her chin to her right armpit. "It hasn't been there long, but it's really been bothering me."

The cut was actually on the side of her breast. And it had been made that morning when Cain had carefully given her a superficial gash with his hidden blade.

She thought she heard Davis suck in a breath, but he didn't say anything as he turned to get some sort of disinfectant salve from a medical kit. Very gently he wiped down the cut and then spread the salve over the wound.

When he accidentally grazed her hard nipple with the side of his hand, Riana sucked in a sharp breath and arched her back slightly.

The second time he brushed her nipple, she wasn't sure it was an accident.

"Does he…," Davis began, clearing his throat after his voice cracked. His face was even more flushed now, and there was a barely suppressed smolder in his eyes. "Does he hurt you?"

She didn't bother asking who he was talking about. "Do you mean does he beat me or anything? No. He doesn't."

Davis's eyes shifted briefly back up to her eyes. "He doesn't?"

She managed to shape a little smile, hoping it looked like mutual understanding based on the skepticism in his voice. "He really doesn't. He thinks of me as his. He likes to… to make sure everyone knows I'm his. But he doesn't want me damaged."

He'd bandaged the cut and smoothed it one last time, letting his hand linger on her breast just a second too long. "Where was the other cut?"

Riana swallowed hard and worried her lower lip with her teeth.

Davis's brows drew together. "Where is it?" His voice was gentler than before.

"Down there," Riana whispered, nodding down between her legs. "He… he cut me."

Davis's hand jerked visibly. "What?"

"He cut me," she explained. "When he was… was shaving me."

His stared down at her smooth, shaven groin. "He shaves you?" He sounded absolutely horrified.

"He likes me to… to look a certain way."

The cut next to her pussy had been Riana's idea. Cain had wanted to just use the one gash near her breast, but Riana had been worried that wouldn't be enough to distract Davis long enough for the time they needed.

She didn't have as much confidence in her charms as Cain had.

Cain had not been at all happy about the idea of cutting her in that spot, and he'd been even less happy about the idea of Davis looking, touching her down there.

But Riana had insisted—wanting to use every advantage they possibly could—and in the end, strategy and necessity had outweighed Cain's instinctive protectiveness.

Secretly, Riana had been a tiny bit pleased by this evidence of his possessiveness of her, but she tried not to dwell on such an unworthy reaction to such unnatural circumstances.

With an almost delicate touch, Davis wiped the cut, which was genuinely uncomfortable, in the crease between her inner thigh and her pussy.

She gasped at the first contact and arched her spine to push up her breasts again, hoping to distract him and thus stall even more.

"Does it hurt? I'm sorry." Davis's hand was shaking a little now.

If something didn't happen soon, then Riana was going to have to descend to more dramatic tactics. The next step would be to put her in that tube, and then Cain would have a much harder time getting to her.

She was just thinking through what kind of dramatic tactics she would use when there was a sudden, loud crack of noise. The bang was so loud and so sudden—accompanied by an ominous shaking—that Riana cried out in real astonishment.

"What the…" Davis's head jerked up, and he looked around in vague confusion. He must not be quite at his full thinking capacity after what Hall had done to him since his reactions were very slow.

"What was that?" she gasped.

"I don't…" Another shaking—it felt kind of like an earthquake—and alarms started to blare from every side. "Damn it."

He turned toward the door. "I'll be back."

She knew he'd be back, but she wasn't planning to be here when he returned.

Cain's device had caused some sort of explosion. It wasn't a bomb exactly—at least not as she'd ever understood explosive devices—but it blasted one of the walls of the prison hold. Not enough to cause structural damage, to flood the Hold with poisoned water or cause massive devastation. The foundations and reinforcement of the building structure were far too solid for that. Nothing Cain could create with spare parts could possibly do more than scratch the surface of the wall.

The damage was only superficial—a loud noise, a lot of rumbling, some dislocated concrete and metal. Since he'd planted it in the public bathroom, it should also mess up the plumbing.

At most, it would be a temporary inconvenience—as the prison staff scrambled to repair the damage. The device was never intended to forcefully blast a way out of the Hold.

It just provided a distraction.

The explosion was certain to cause chaos in the prison however—and that chaos could very easily turn into a riot as the prison staff attempted to maintain order as well as assess and repair the damage.

The chaos would also give Cain and Hall a chance to get out.

At least that was the plan.

She wasn't sure how they would do so. The men hadn't even been sure. They'd just have to take advantage of the chaos and somehow manage to slip out, using the bracelet they'd taken from Davis that was supposed to unlock the doors.

No one was as strong as Cain, and Hall had his special gift. Surely between the two of them and the bracelet, they could do it.

If not, it had all been for nothing, and she'd be taken through the long, arduous medical tests and returned to the prison this evening—where she and Cain would spend the rest of their days penned up like animals.

She waited, still trapped by the manacles on the table. Cain should be here soon. Any time. He'd said to wait for him, that he would come for her. She knew he'd meant it.

If he didn't come, it would mean he'd failed. Or he was dead.

She was just mentally flailing at that thought when the doors slid open and Cain ran into the room, sweating, his shirt torn, a gash under one eye, and holding a gun he must have taken off a guard.

He'd clearly had to fight to get to her.

She gave a little sob of relief as he released the manacles and helped her off the table. She kind of collapsed against him, and he gave her a quick, hard hug, interrupted when Hall ducked his head in the room. "No time for that. We need to move now."

Hall had evidently been fighting too. Blood was smeared in his hair, and he was holding his arm strangely.

Riana grabbed her clothes and was trying to pull them on quickly as Cain tugged her toward the door. "So the bracelet thing worked?" she asked.

"So far."

The three of them started toward the control center. A guard appeared in the doorway—evidently left on duty when the rest went to see about the crisis—so Cain calmly shot him in the shoulder, sending him flopping to the floor.

Riana hugged herself—feeling self-conscious and jittery—as Cain walked over to the control panel. There was a bank of display screens, on which appeared surveillance images of the prison. It appeared to be chaos, with rioting prisoners and scrambling guards, just as they'd hoped.

"I'm opening the transport docking doors," Cain said curtly, pulling down a lever and flicking a switch. "It looks like there's a three-minute delay—another safety precaution, I assume—so we'll need to stay here so no one comes in and cancels the opening."

Riana's mind was such a blur of anxiety, adrenalin, and excitement that she could barely process that this was actually happening. "I can't believe this is working."

"We're not out of here yet," Hall said. His eyes ran up and down her body. "You might want to finish putting your clothes on." He gave her a little quirk of a smile. "Not that I'm complaining."

Cain made a guttural sound, and Riana pulled her top on since she'd only gotten her trousers on before.

Cain watched her but only in an impersonal way. After the quick hug he'd given her earlier, he didn't even seem glad to see her. He was vigilantly focused on their plan and wasn't wasting any time with warm looks or appreciation.

"So everything went as we planned?" he asked gruffly when she'd come over to stand beside him.

"Yeah." She kept her voice low so Hall, across the room, couldn't hear her. He'd known the plan too, but it still felt too personal to talk about with him. "Perfect. For a while I was afraid he was going to drop his pants or something, but the explosion came in time."

"How far did he get?" If possible, Cain's voice was even gruffer than before.

"All he got to do was feel my breasts and brush up against my girly parts." She let out a textured sigh and felt an uncomfortable twisting in her belly. "He was getting excited. I actually feel kind of bad for him."

Cain stiffened beside her. "Do you?"

Noticing his tense face, Riana frowned. "You're not going to get weird on me, are you? This was part of the plan."

His mouth pressed into a tight line, and he didn't respond.

Riana stewed, wondering what was going on in his head and pretty sure she'd be annoyed by it until Cain said, "There. The doors are opening. Let's get out of here."

As they ran for the docking bay, two more guards appeared in the hall, yelling, "Hey!" as they realized there were escaped prisoners.

Cain knocked out one before the man could even raise the gun, and Hall grabbed the gun from the other one and slammed it into his head.

Then more appeared—so many that Riana's mind blurred over in fear. There were a few shots from both sides that must have missed, but they were in such tight quarters in the hall that they had to resort to hand-to-hand combat. As Cain and Hall grappled with several guards, Riana managed to get a gun from one who'd been knocked out, and she used it to level a hard blow against the back of the head of the man who was going after Cain.

The impact of the blow jarred her whole body, but at least the man went down.

She was still trying to process the scene when Cain grabbed her arm again, dragging her down the hall to the docking station doors.

There, Cain raised the mechanism from the bracelet to unlock the door, which opened directly into the transport. Opening the docking doors flooded the bay with poisonous water, so transports had to attach directly to the station.

After that it was almost easy. The docking doors were starting to close again—as a guard must have seen they were opened and hurried to shut them—but they closed too slowly to matter. They took their places at the controls of the transport, and Hall started the engine, unhooked from the station, and pulled the transport out into the ocean before the doors could close all the way.

The transport was not one of the Coalition's sleek newer vessels. It was clunky and battered, and it lurched and groaned as Hall steered it. But it moved. And it started rising toward the surface of the ocean with only a few more creaks and sputters.

It was going to get them out of this hellhole. Off the planet completely.

As far as Riana was concerned, it was a wonderful, beautiful craft.

She was silent as they emerged from the ocean and Hall adjusted the controls to launch the transport off the surface of the water and into the thin atmosphere of Genus 6.

When they'd broken through the gravitational force, Riana let out a long exhalation. She felt weird. And shaky. And kind of sick.

Cain glanced over at her. "You okay?"

She blinked, having a hard time processing anything. Cain was bleeding from his shoulder too, she managed to realize. "Huh?"

"You look white," Hall said, looking over at her from his steering. One of his eyes was swollen shut. "Are you feeling all right?"

"I don't know," she admitted. "I can't believe this is happening." She put a hand on her stomach. "Did we really get away?"

Cain's eyes softened a little as they rested on her face. "We're getting there."

"It all happened so fast," she mumbled. "And with this clunky transport, I guess I'm feeling kind of dizzy."

"That's natural."

She tried to frown at him, but she was trembling too much. "You don't look—" She broke off, groaning as she felt a sudden wave of nausea. Then with a flash of panic, she realized what was going to happen.

She fumbled with her safety belt and went to grab a waste container just as her stomach started to heave. She vomited painfully. A stark physical reaction that seemed to be in response—not just to the jerky motion of the transport and the shift in atmosphere and gravity—but also to the adrenaline high of the past few hours and the trauma of the past two months.

Feeling better after she threw up, she wiped her mouth with her hand.

"All right?" Cain asked, a flicker of worry on his stoic face.

Burning with embarrassment, she slanted him a sheepish look. "Yeah. Just pretend you guys didn't see that, all right?"

Hall laughed, and Cain grunted—a grunt she recognized as both relief and amusement. He said, "I didn't see a thing."

Riana stood up, feeling more grounded now that she'd become used to the motion of the transport. "Are they going to chase us?"

"They'll make at least a cursory pursuit, but I don't think they'll call for any help. That would mean admitting they let prisoners escape. They'll probably just count us among the dead from the riot. You know what the Coalition is like—let things slide unless it directly impacts them. We need to dump this transport and find a safer spacecraft as soon as we can, though, just in case they decide to be thorough."

"Genus 5 is less than an hour away," Hall said. "I'll take us there. The capital is a big city. Anything goes there. We can get lost there easily enough."

Cain nodded in agreement.

"Sounds good." She was about to take her seat again when she thought of something else. "So we have an hour?"

"Just about. Why? Did you want to take a nap?"

"No. Too jittery for that yet. But there's probably a shower in the head. If you don't need me to help…"

Cain smiled, an uncharacteristically soft look on his face. "We've got it covered up here. Go take a shower."

Riana did.

The shower was old-fashioned, a little rusty, and wasn't particularly clean. But it had been two months since Riana had been able to take one.

With the exception of having sex with Cain, nothing had ever felt better in her life.

～

When they landed on Genus 5, they left the transport in a public docking station, and Hall did his persuasion thing and got enough money to buy them a meal and a change of clothes. They went to a rather sleazy bar that evening, and they used the remaining money to join a card game. By the end of the night, they'd won a rickety spacecraft—this one safely anonymous—and enough money for fuel and adequate provisions.

Riana wasn't surprised by their success at gambling.

No one could bluff better than Cain, and Hall could make people do whatever he wanted them to do.

She'd felt awkward and uncertain ever since they landed. Hall was planning to take off on his own once he got to some planet where a friend of his lived. He would start up his life again, doing any sort of freelance work that made him money. But she wasn't sure what Cain's plans were once they were safely away. He would have had every right to dump her on the first convenient occasion instead of hauling her around, but she certainly didn't suggest it.

That evening, they got rooms in a hole-in-the-wall lodging house that didn't ask for identification, and since they'd only gotten two rooms, she assumed she was sleeping with Cain.

They both took showers before bed, and Riana spent a long time combing the tangles out of her hair. But they didn't talk much. Cain seemed closed off and brooding, and everything felt so strange, unnatural.

Cain didn't even smell like himself. He smelled like soap. It seemed foreign and unreal.

"Is your shoulder okay?" she asked. He'd been bleeding there earlier.

"Yeah. Shallow wound. Nothing serious."

"Do you want me to bandage it up?"

"I already took care of it." He was wearing a T-shirt with sleeves. She'd never seen him wearing sleeves before.

"Okay," she said, swallowing hard. She wanted to say something else—something about how odd she felt, how different things were, how she felt like he was slipping through her fingers. But he wasn't in a talkative mood, and she was terrified of hearing the truth, so she didn't end up saying anything but, "Good night."

Maybe he would roll over on top of her the way he often did. Maybe with sex things would feel more natural.

But he didn't make any advances at all. He just said, "Good night," back to her and turned off the light.

It felt like he was a stranger beside her, and she realized with the bleak weight of impending knowledge that what had been so good inside the prison might not last now that they were out. What she desperately wanted, needed from him might not be a possibility.

Freedom might mean she had lost him.

It wasn't pitch-black in the room the way it had always been in the Hold at night, but she still felt lonely and scared for a long time before she finally went to sleep.

~

She smelled Cain as she woke up.

It was just a faint whiff—not the way she'd always been surrounded by the scent of him on waking—but it was distinct, unmistakable, deeply known.

It was Cain, and she'd know him anywhere.

She rolled toward the smell of him as she gradually woke up until she could feel his body beneath her hands. She breathed deeply, comforted by the familiar scent of him.

"What are you doing?" he asked, his voice gruff, fully awake.

"Smelling you," she mumbled, obviously not quite in her right mind yet.

"Sorry. I can take another shower."

"No." She reached out for him groggily, sighing with pleasure as he wrapped his arms around her and pulled her against him. "I like it."

He chuckled and slid his hands down her back until he was cupping her bottom. "I'm not sure what to think about that."

"It's strange—being out," she admitted, nuzzling his chest and breathing him in.

He exhaled deeply. "I know."

She moved against him and felt that he was hard, his erection trapped between their bodies. A tension unclenched in her chest at the recognition. He still wanted her. At least that hadn't changed.

She rubbed herself against him slowly until he moaned, low in his throat. Then he grabbed her face and pulled her into a deep kiss.

They kissed for a long time, moving their bodies against each other. It felt so different—with clean skin, clean hair—but the hard tension in his body, the urgency in his touch hadn't changed.

With one hand, he stroked her hair as they kissed, and with the other he caressed one of her thighs. It wasn't long until she was deeply aroused, whimpering slightly as desire pulsed all through her.

"Cain, please," she gasped, pulling her mouth away at last. "I need you. Now."

He released a muffled groan and rolled them over so she was on her back and he was positioned between her thighs. They fumbled with their clothes, and he used his hand to align himself at her entrance, and then he was sinking inside.

Her pussy clung to his hard length, and she arched up in pleasure at the penetration. "Cain."

He pushed a few times against her—just small, involuntary thrusts. And he said one breathless word with each push. "Yes. Baby. Riana."

She arched up again, loving the sound of his voice, the feel of his need. She wrapped her legs around him and held on to him with her thighs and her arms. She kept breathing out his name as she rocked beneath him, matching his rhythm by instinct as much as practice. She couldn't seem to stop.

Then he was kissing her again, even as their motion became more urgent, and it felt like they were truly joined, truly together, truly one. Her chest was aching with it as the pleasure released inside her, and she arched her neck, breaking the kiss and crying out softly as her body shook through the climax.

"Fuck, yeah," he muttered, pushing against her contractions. "Baby, I love when you come."

He was sweating now, and he smelled more like Cain than ever. And she'd come down enough to watch and feel as he froze, the release breaking on his face, before it washed over him with palpable pleasure.

She held on as he came inside her, and she gathered him to her when he started to relax.

He lay on top of her for a minute, his weight heavy and hot and loved.

"That was so good," she breathed after a minute, needing to say something, desperately wanting to hear from him some sort of reflection of her own feelings.

"Yeah," he muttered, nuzzling her neck.

She waited, but he didn't say anything else.

Maybe it was just sex to him. Maybe it was just a physical release. Maybe he wanted to go back to his real life and cut any ties from the memory of the nightmare year he'd spent in the prison.

Who could blame him, after all? Relationships formed in crisis weren't supposed to last.

She wasn't going to make him feel guilty. He'd more than lived up to his side of their deal. He hadn't just kept her safe and taken care of her while they were in the Hold. He'd managed to get them both out. She wasn't going to make him feel bad if he didn't want to have her around for the rest of his life.

The idea of living the rest of her life without him upset her so much that she suddenly had to get some space. She squirmed slightly until he rolled off her, and then she tucked herself into a ball under the covers, telling herself to hold it together.

Cain had a good heart, no matter how he tried to hide it. Even a year in the prison hadn't managed to beat it out of him. If he knew how sad she was at the thought of losing him, he would feel guilty about it.

It felt like he might be looking at her, but she couldn't take the risk of checking.

Finally he said, "I guess I'll take a shower."

"Okay. I'll take one after you." She thought she managed to sound mostly natural.

She shuddered and shook after Cain got up and went to the bathroom until she'd controlled the emotion.

There was a knock on the door a few minutes after she heard the shower come on. She sat up with a jerk, surprised and momentarily terrified.

They'd seen a couple of guards from the prison yesterday evening at the public docking station. Evidently, they'd made a search for them after all.

Maybe they'd found them.

"It's me," Hall's voice came through the door.

Relieved, Riana threw her clothes on and went to open the door.

Hall was fully dressed and grinning—breathtakingly handsome despite his still swollen eye. She pitied the girl who Hall made a real move on. The poor thing wouldn't have a chance.

"I found a ride," he said, glancing behind her and evidently realizing that Cain was in the bathroom. "I think we'll be safer going our ways now."

"Oh, okay." Riana agreed he was probably right, but she was kind of sorry to see Hall go. She felt strangely close to this mysterious, charismatic, incredibly attractive man. "Who's your ride?"

"Someone going the same direction as me." He lifted his eyebrows. "She was happy to give me a lift."

"I bet she was."

"So I'm taking off. Take care of yourself," Hall said, leaning down to kiss her cheek. "Thanks for picking me out of the herd and giving me an escape route."

He'd said he was going to kill himself if he'd stayed much longer in the Hold. She was absolutely sure it was true.

In a fleeting thought, she decided the world would have been lesser if he had.

"Thank you," she said with a smile. "We couldn't have gotten out without your help. You're going to be okay?"

"Of course. I know how to take care of myself."

"Don't get in trouble again."

"I'm always in trouble." He gave her his characteristic grin. "I'd tell you to take care of yourself too, but I think someone already has the job covered."

"I... don't know about that," Riana said a little primly since she wasn't at all sure his assumption about her and Cain was true, and it really wasn't Hall's business anyway.

He chuckled and lowered his face to murmur, "You might not know, but I do. I read his feelings, remember? And I've never felt anything like it before—the way he feels for you."

She stared at him breathlessly, a thrill rippling through her at the words. "Really?"

He nodded. "If I felt that deeply for a woman, I'd be absolutely terrified." He glanced over her shoulder at the closed door of the bathroom. "Tell him good-bye from me. And thank you. And that he has nothing to feel guilty about."

"What?" Riana asked, trying to sort out exactly what he was saying.

"Just tell him," Hall said. Then he kissed her cheek again and turned to leave. But he added as he walked down the hall, "You can trust me."

She stared after him for a minute, and she was still staring when the bathroom door opened.

"What's going on?" Cain asked, low and hoarse.

Riana closed the door. "Hall. He got a ride to that planet he was heading for, so he came by say good-bye."

"Oh. You didn't want to go with him?"

She sucked in a sharp breath, turning to stare at Cain. "Why would I?"

He gave a half shrug as he pulled on the pair of pants he'd bought the day before.

She was confused and emotional and flooded with far too many unanswered questions.

Where was Cain planning to go now anyway? When were they going to discuss future plans?

Would he want to go back to his old life and forget about her completely?

All the questions made her stomach knot as she watched Cain pull on a shirt.

She was breathing deeply and telling herself not to panic when he asked, "What's the matter?"

"Nothing."

"You look kind of shaky. Are you feeling sick again?" he asked, his face softening slightly in concern. "After being cooped up under the ocean for so long, it could just be the change in press—"

"I'm fine," she interrupted. "I'm not sick."

He lowered his brow as if confused by her tone.

Trying to hide her nerves, she asked, "Do you think we're safe to be out in public? Since we saw them here... I mean, since they came after us after all?"

"It was probably more of a gesture toward pursuit than the real thing. They don't seem to have called in reinforcements. We aren't enemies of the state, and they won't want the publicity of admitting that anyone managed to escape from one of their prison planets. Occasionally, convicts have made escapes before, but the news is always hushed up. It will be easy enough to cover up—with the explosion and rioting that followed. They'll just announce that we died in the chaos. The other prisoners will probably believe it, and no one else will even know to care."

It made sense. And knowing how the Coalition functioned primarily to cover its own ass, Riana realized that was exactly what would happen in this.

"So what are you going to do now?" Riana's voice cracked slightly as she asked, but her emotions and confusion were rising up again.

Hall had said Cain cared about her. Surely he wouldn't have lied about that.

"I'm going home."

"Oh."

She had no idea where his home was. Where he lived. What he did. Who his family was.

He might have a wife and kids.

He might be anything.

"Where would you like me to take you?" He'd turned slightly, like he was about to head back into the bathroom.

Riana swallowed hard and tried to think. "I'm not sure. Since I'm a convict and they know my name, I can hardly go back to the University. Even if they aren't going to try to track me down, I can't really just appear back on Earth and demand my old job back."

"No, but it's not difficult to take on a new identity these days. I would have to myself, but I refused to give them my name, so they never officially knew who I was."

Once technology had advanced to an extent that fingerprint identification was obsolete, the Coalition had turned to other methods of keeping track of people. But the Coalition was too vast to keep records on everyone, so only those born in Coalition hospitals or those on staff with the Coalition had their genetic identity on record. Those born on underdeveloped planets like Cain's could easily avoid getting tagged in such a way. It didn't make a difference in the criminal system since they imprisoned people whether they had a real name or not, but she could understand now why Cain had been stubborn about this. He would have lost his chance to go home again otherwise.

After a reflective pause, Cain continued, "You can probably forge identification and credentials without too much trouble and get a new job—maybe even doing archeology. I'm sure you have friends or family who could help you."

Growing dread was a sickening weight in her gut as she tried to imagine starting her life over now. Alone.

Without Cain.

But Hall had said Cain had feelings for her.

"I don't have any family left," she murmured, staring down at her hands.

"Friends? Boyfriend?"

"I've always kept to myself, but I'll figure it out. There's no way I can thank you for everything—"

Cain put up an impatient hand. "None of that."

"But—"

His lips twisted with some sort of suppressed emotion. "I haven't been selfless. The way I've used you—"

Riana almost choked. "What? What do you mean?"

Cain turned to stare at her again. "I took advantage of you. We both know that. You were helpless. And I used that to fuck you the way I wanted—"

"No!" she exclaimed, horrified by the very idea, by the fact that Cain believed that about what had happened between them. She suddenly understood what Hall had meant when he'd said to tell Cain not to feel guilty. "No. I went into it willingly. It was an even trade. A consensual agreement. And after the first time, it didn't... it didn't..."

Cain leaned forward, his eyes scanning her face intensely. "It didn't what?"

She gave up even trying to retain the last remnants of her pride. He might as well know the whole truth. "After the first time, it didn't feel like a trade. I mean, I didn't think of it as something I had to do. I wanted to. And I thought... I guess I thought you understood that."

Cain was silent for a long time.

Outside the prison, he appeared more human. He was still powerful, stoic, intimidating, but he didn't seem quite so primal in his bearing and demeanor. He was just a man, after all. A strong, masculine, eminently capable one. But a man.

A man who looked confused and a little uncertain right now.

Finally he said, "I knew you enjoyed it physically, but you can't tell me you would have taken up with me had you not been forced into it by circumstances."

Riana narrowed her eyes. "Would you have taken up with me?"

"That's not the same, Riana." He almost never said her name, and the sound of it now made her belly clench with emotion. "I was the one with the power there."

"You had strength—yes. But I chose you, remember? I picked you out because I liked what I saw in you. You never took me against my will. So if you've been carrying around this stupid guilt for all these weeks, you can give it the fuck up!" Her voice was sharp, and for some reason she wanted to strangle him.

Here she was, terrified that he was going to dump her and go on with his life. And break her heart in the process.

And he was brooding about something so irrational and unnecessary.

"Oh," Cain murmured, his lips twitching slightly. She recognized his expression of amusement with relief. "My mistake."

After a moment, his brows drew together and he asked, "So what exactly are you saying?"

Put on the spot, Riana just blurted out the truth. "I want to stay with you." Blushing furiously as Cain gaped at her, she tried to backpedal a little. "I mean, I think there's something between us. Or could be."

"And you think it will last now that we're out?"

"I don't know for sure, but why shouldn't it? I don't want to give you up just because we were thrown together in an unnatural situation. Maybe these feelings will fade away once things go back to normal. But maybe they won't. I... I like you. And I'd like to stick around. Unless you have a wife or—"

"I don't have a wife," Cain interrupted, his voice sounding a little strangled. His face twisted slightly, a clear sign of emotion on his usually stoic countenance. "Of course I want you to stay with me. I've spent the past twelve hours talking myself out of throwing you over my shoulder and carrying you home with me. I just thought now that you finally have choices you'd want to get on with your life."

It took her a minute to process his words. Then to realize what they meant.

When Riana finally understood that he felt the same way she did about their relationship, she blazed with joy. She had to hug herself to try to contain it. "I do want to get on with my life. I just want to do it with you." Swallowing hard, she admitted, "I think... I think you're the best thing in my life. And that goes for outside the Hold, not just in it."

She saw something flare up in Cain's eyes. Something she'd never seen there long enough to recognize before. It took her breath away. "Me too," he muttered, low and hoarse.

She wanted to grab him and kiss him and then decided there was no reason not to. So she launched herself at him, wrapping her arms around his neck.

Cain didn't seem inclined to let her go.

They'd been kissing fairly regularly for the past month, but it had never been as good as this.

After a minute of embracing with hungry exhilaration, Riana asked, "So where exactly do you live?"

Cain idly rubbed her thigh as if he couldn't touch her enough. "On the outskirts of the Sient galaxy. That's where I was born, and I still have a home there."

"What do you do anyway? I've always wanted to know."

He chuckled. "So why didn't you ask me?" Before she could shape her outraged objection to this insolence, he went on, "I have a ranch."

Riana's mouth fell open. "A ranch? Like a real ranch? With cows and everything? I thought beef was all mass produced now."

"There's still a specialized market for the real thing. I inherited the ranch from my father. The planet is mostly undeveloped." He darted her a slightly nervous look. "It's not very exciting. I'm not sure it's what you'll be used to. There's only one city on the entire planet. Most of the land is agricultural. Maybe you should check it out before you commit yourself to staying with me. There's nothing but grass, some rolling hills, big skies."

Riana squeezed her arms around Cain's neck and whispered, "Sounds about perfect to me."

That answer seemed to please him immensely, and he claimed her mouth in a long kiss. After he'd suitably expressed his appreciation, he stroked her bottom and murmured, "Let's not move too quickly. We'll call it a visit at first so you can see what it's like without any pressure. If it seems like a place you'd like to stay and if your... your feelings for me don't start to change now that you have real options, then we'll consider it a more permanent arrangement."

Riana had no fears of her feelings for him changing. She'd never been more sure of anything in her life.

But all she said was, "Sounds good to me."

They stayed like that for a while—sometimes kissing, sometimes just holding each other—until Riana asked out of the blue, "So what did you get convicted of anyway?"

Cain let out a surprised burst of laughter. "About time you ask me that. Getting worried that you've just hooked up with a serial killer?"

Riana waved away that nonsense. "Not once did I ever think such a thing about you. I know you're not a killer."

He'd been nuzzling her hair, but now he shifted to murmur against her ear, "And how did you know that?"

"You act tough," she began. When she noticed his expression, she rephrased. "You are tough. You were stronger than anyone else. But you weren't vicious, and you didn't hurt people for fun. You didn't shoot that guard to kill when we escaped."

Cain just made a grunt.

"And I was wondering if Asp was the first man you'd ever killed."

He didn't answer for a long time, during which Riana's heart beat frantically, afraid she'd pushed too far. Then he finally admitted, "He was."

"So what crime did you commit?"

His face twisted reluctantly.

Frowning, Riana persisted, "How bad could it be? I figured it was smuggling or something. I didn't know you were a rancher, and since you seemed to have traveled so much, I thought maybe you had a ship and bought and sold black-market—"

"No. Nothing that exciting. You'll need to ask Hall about that kind of thing. I did have a ship for the business. It was always breaking down and I'd have to fix it, which is actually how I knew enough to put together that device. But that was only out of necessity. I actually prefer not to travel at all, and I'd recently found a partner who was going to take over the sales end of things for the ranch. But I couldn't stay there all the time. I was basically by myself, and there wasn't a chance for... for..."

Riana suddenly understood his awkward expression. She choked on a burst of laughter. "So you had to make trips to the galaxy hot spots so you could have some fun and find a woman or two to fuck?"

His expression affirmed this as the truth.

While Riana didn't like the idea of Cain fucking anyone but her, she could hardly blame the man for needing to find some physical release now and then. And she was kind of glad he hadn't had a serious girlfriend or someone he had feelings for.

Maybe it was selfish—since it meant he'd been lonely for a long time—but she liked that she was the first woman he'd cared for like this.

"Anyway," Cain admitted, his voice even gruffer than normal. "I made the mistake of sleeping with the wrong woman. Apparently she was the mistress of a Coalition commander and..."

Riana gasped, horrified and disbelieving at once. "You got sent to that hellhole just because you fucked some tramp?"

He gave her a wry look. Like her, he seemed to have turned to bitter irony as the only way to handle living in Coalition space. "Almost as good as trespassing, isn't it?"

She wasn't sure if she wanted to cry or laugh, so she settled for squeezing him in her arms. "My God, Cain. And you were there for more than a year. How did you stand it?"

He was holding on to her so tightly she was afraid her ribs might crack. But she didn't want him to let go.

He wasn't a sentimental man, and he wasn't an openly emotional one. But she understood him just the same.

And right now he was making it clear that he needed desperately to hold on to her for fear he would lose what was so important to him.

That would have been enough. The admission she could feel in his grip. But to her surprise he managed to shape his feelings in words.

He muttered, "I wouldn't have made it without you.

EPILOGUE

Riana woke up alone.

The bed was familiar now—big, clean, and comfortable. And there was faint light shining dimly from the hallway.

She never slept in pitch-darkness anymore.

But when she rolled over and opened her eyes, she saw the other side of the bed was empty. The covers were warm and rumpled from where he'd been sleeping, but Cain was no longer in bed.

She wasn't surprised or particularly concerned. She knew immediately where he was.

Sometimes she just went back to sleep when she woke up and found he was missing. But this was the third night this week. So she rolled out of bed and padded barefoot out of the house.

Both moons were nearly full, and the night was clear, so there was plenty of light illuminating the expansive yard and the sloped fields surrounding the house. Cain's ranch was vast, and it had taken her weeks to grow familiar with the endless stretches of land. But she knew where she was going now.

The soft grass was cool beneath her feet, and she wished she'd put a wrap around her sleeveless nightgown before she'd come outside. The weather here was milder than on Earth, but the evenings were brisk this time of year.

She found Cain exactly where she'd expected him to be. He was stretched out on a blanket, on the top of a hill behind the main house. He didn't have a shirt on, but he was wearing the soft, pull-on pants he usually slept in. His arms were crossed behind his head, and he was staring up at the stars in the sky.

He didn't turn his head or speak as she approached, but when she lay down beside him, he reached out for her, pulling her snugly against his side and keeping his arm around her.

"Did you have another one?" she murmured, feeling like she needed to speak softly so she wouldn't disturb the quiet serenity of the evening.

"Yeah."

Cain had been having nightmares semiregularly since they'd escaped. He might go weeks without one, but then something—usually stress or an emotional disturbance—would trigger them again.

His nightmares were always the same. Being trapped in a small space in the dark. Being helpless to get out, to respond, to move.

Riana's two months in the prison had traumatized her as well. But Cain had been locked up a year longer than her.

"That's the third time this week." She stroked his chest, enjoying the feel of the firm flesh, hard muscles, and coarse hair. His body was still as tight and muscular as it had been in prison. He was a physical man, and he worked hard every day on this ranch.

Riana worked hard too, but it was work she'd grown to love as much as Cain did. He raised a kind of hybrid cattle that had been brought here from Earth several generations back. He had horses too, and Riana had delighted in learning to ride.

There were a lot of planets like this in Coalition space—on the outskirts, overlooked by those in authority, rustic and backward in the popular conception.

But Riana loved the simplicity and the natural beauty—especially since the natural beauty of Earth and the major planets of the Coalition had been used up ages ago. And she also loved how far removed this planet was from the notice of the Coalition. She felt at peace here. And at home. For the first time in her life.

"I'm sorry if I woke you up." Cain's voice was low and gruff, but his hand was gentle as it stroked her hair. "I try to be quiet."

"You didn't wake me up. I think I just know when you're not in bed with me."

"Sometimes I sleep better out here."

It wasn't difficult to understand why. If his fear was enclosure, being boxed in, then the vast fields, endless sky, and fresh air of this spot was as far from that as possible. Sometimes Cain just couldn't stand to be inside.

When a night was as gorgeous as this one, Riana could hardly blame him.

So she scooted up and draped herself on him, caressing the strong lines of his face with one hand. "You haven't had three nightmares in one week for a long time. Is there anything you want to tell me?"

Something must be troubling him. He would always be the strong, silent type—and he'd never spill out all his feelings like she did—but they'd made a lot of progress in their relationship over the past eight months. And he was always honest with her when she asked him directly.

He gazed up at her, his blue eyes reflecting an expression she saw a lot now—made up of tenderness, possessiveness, and something like awe. "You're so beautiful." He reached up to push her dark curls back from where they'd been grazing his chest. She'd let her hair grow long and washed it sometimes twice a day.

Riana smiled although she was deeply touched by the simple compliment. "Don't try to distract me with flattery," she told him. "Has something been troubling you? Does it have something to do with this?"

Placing her left hand on his chest, she stared down at the ring on her finger, the one he'd given her last week.

Presenting a woman with a diamond ring for an engagement was an old-fashioned custom that wasn't followed by most couples anymore—the general consensus labeling the little ritual outdated and out of keeping with Coalition values and sensibilities.

But Cain was an old-fashioned guy. And when he'd asked her to marry him last week, he'd given her the diamond ring she was wearing.

It was the best gift Riana had ever received.

Cain picked up her hand from his chest and pressed a kiss into her palm. "I'm not getting cold feet if that's what you think."

"I didn't think that." She shifted above him, her hip grazing his groin. And she was surprised and pleased to feel that he had grown a little hard—just from having her body draped over his. "But I wondered if you were worried about something related to us."

He didn't respond immediately. Just idly stroked her hair. Then finally he murmured, "I think you know what it is."

"I do," she admitted, leaning down to press a little kiss just to the side of his mouth. "But do you think you can tell me anyway?"

He closed his eyes and took a deep breath in a conscious effort to break down the defenses of stoicism that came naturally to him and that had solidified to a frightening extent during his experience in the Hold.

But he'd come a long way since then, and now he told her the truth. "I still don't think I deserve you. I don't deserve to be so happy. After the way I acted there—after what I became there."

Riana exhaled discreetly, relieved he'd finally gotten it said. "That's silly," she whispered, adjusting to rest her cheek on his chest, thinking he'd feel more comfortable talking about this if she wasn't staring at him.

"I know. But sometimes I felt... like an animal there."

She frowned, caressing the side of his flat belly. "You were not an animal. I saw who you really were. I knew you were strong, but I could also see your... your humanness. That's why I chose you."

"Maybe you saw a glimmer of it, but there wasn't much left at that point. When I first saw you, I wanted you so much. You were so beautiful and brave and untouched by the grim reality of the Hold. You were the only light I'd seen in that whole dark year. I wanted it, so I just took it."

He'd never shared so much about how he'd felt the first time he'd seen her or what his motivation in coming to fight for her had been. Despite the seriousness of their conversation, Riana was moved by his admission. And she felt a little thrill of girly delight that she'd provoked such a reaction in this powerful man.

"You didn't take it," she objected. "I offered it to you. Would you have come out of your cell at all if I hadn't let you know I wanted you to?"

"No," he admitted slowly.

"See. Stop beating yourself up. You weren't perfect—you were terse and kind of pushy at first. But I wasn't perfect either. And if I had been in that prison by myself for a year, I would have been a lot less human than you were with me."

He didn't respond, but one of his hands had slid down to cup her bottom.

"I love you, Cain," she murmured, leaning up so she could look down at his face. Her hair spilled down around both of them. "I fell in love with you in that prison. I wouldn't have fallen in love with someone who had just selfishly taken what he wanted from me. You gave as much as you took."

For just a moment his eyes looked almost anguished and desperate. "I hope so."

Realizing that she wasn't going to be able to talk him into believing her, she leaned down to kiss him—deeply, softly, lovingly. He responded immediately, his hands clutching at her and his mouth opening hungrily to hers.

When she broke off the kiss, she murmured against his mouth, "Are you happy, Cain?"

"You know I'm happy. That's where all the guilt comes from."

She kissed him again, brushing her fingers along the tight skin of his scalp, feeling the light texture of the dark hair he still shaved close. "How happy are you?"

He didn't want to release her lips, but when he finally broke off to breathe, he said thickly, "I feel like every dream

I've ever had—even the ones I never knew I wanted—has come true."

She wanted to melt from pure joy and tenderness. She rubbed her body against his hard one, realizing he had grown more erect. "Me too," she breathed, kissing little lines around his face. "That's how happy I am too. I was lonely and aimless all my life. And you're the one who has helped me change that. If I'm this happy to be with you, why should you ever feel guilty about it?"

Cain had grabbed her hips and was holding her pelvis against his, and she gave a pleased mew at the feel of his erection against her groin. "Good question," he muttered, giving a little buck up into her.

Deciding the time for discussion had passed, Riana pulled her little nightgown off over her head so she was naked to the open air and night sky. Cain reached up to cup and fondle her breasts as she pushed down his pants to free his cock.

She was fully aroused by the time she lined up over him and slid down to sheathe his erection with her pussy. She rode him slowly for a minute, rocking over his prone form and taking sensual enjoyment in the feel of his cock sliding inside her.

He lay still and watched her move, his eyes never leaving her face and bare body.

After a few minutes though, his body grew tighter and his hands closed down hard around her hips. "Riana," he said thickly, "can you come, baby?"

She didn't really care if she came or not. Her heart was too full of everything else to feel particularly urgent about an orgasm. So she leaned over and whispered, "If you want to take over, you can."

Evidently, Cain wanted to take over. He flipped them over, holding her body in place so his cock didn't slip out of her slick channel. Then he began to thrust from between her legs. When she bent her knees, he grabbed them and pushed them closer to her chest.

Riana gasped at feeling him inside her from this new angle and from the way he was forcefully shaking her body against the soft ground.

Cain's face had broken out in a sheen of perspiration, and he was gazing down at her with hunger and love. "So good," he gritted out. "So beautiful. So good. Love you so much."

She whimpered at his words and at the intensifying sensations at her center. She knew how much he loved her, needed her, adored her—and she'd never known what it was for someone to feel that way for her before. The way their love had begun might have made things more complicated, but it didn't change the reality of it now.

And she was going to come. Knowing that he loved her. And knowing that she loved him.

Her body tightened in preparation as his thrusting became fast and hard.

Then she cried out wordlessly as the tension shattered inside her, her body shaking and clenching and pulling him into climax as well.

He claimed her lips as he came, groaning into her mouth and stroking her lips clumsily with his tongue. She kissed him back, still whimpering out the pleasure of her orgasm.

They lay together in a sated tangle of naked limbs until barking interrupted the quiet night.

Riana giggled as she turned her head to see a large brown dog approaching at a dead run.

"You've got to teach him," she said, squeezing Cain with her arms and her legs, "that I'm not in trouble every time I scream."

Cain chuckled too, the delicious vibrations from his amusement shaking his whole body. "He gets worried. Max is a very devoted dog."

Riana had been astonished and delighted when she'd learned that the dog Cain had loved so deeply was still alive. She'd assumed from the way he'd spoken about him in prison that the dog had died.

But Max was still alive. And Cain's business partner— the man who had generously kept the ranch going during Cain's long absence—had also made sure Max was well taken care of.

She'd almost cried that first day when Cain had been reunited with the dog that clearly adored him. She'd had to make a quick exit so Cain wouldn't see her overcome with such silly emotion.

But Max did have an unfortunate habit of coming to the rescue anytime she cried out in some way. If she were genuinely in trouble, it would be very convenient. But most of the times she was crying out with an entirely different emotion.

Max snuffled around Riana's face to assure himself that she was all right. She patted him on the head, and Cain gave him instructions to lie down a short distance from their blanket.

Cain's cock had softened inside her, and his semen was leaking out of her pussy, but she didn't want to move and she didn't want to let go of him. She loved the feel of his weight. Loved the sight of the clear sky—endless and vibrant above her. And she loved the tender security of knowing she was in Cain's arms. She was home.

Out of the blue, she asked, "When you fought Thorn for me and brought me back into your cell, if I had said no, I didn't want to fuck you, would you have forced me anyway? Or would you have thrown me out of the cell if I refused?"

It took Cain a long time to answer. He nuzzled at her neck and breathed deeply as he considered his response. Then he said, "No. I was pretty far gone then, almost an animal, but I would never have forced you or thrown you out."

It was an admission she'd needed Cain to make. For him, not for herself.

She'd already known.

Riana had picked the right man in those first minutes in the Hold. If she'd picked anyone else to protect her, to give her body to, her life would have been utterly different. She wouldn't have had this future.

She wouldn't have Cain.

So she held on to him as tightly as he was holding on to her, knowing neither one would let go.

But she spoke in a teasing, victorious voice that made Cain growl. And all she said was, "That's what I thought."

ABOUT THE AUTHOR

Claire has been writing romance novels since she was twelve years old. She writes contemporary romance and women's fiction with hot sex and real emotion.

She also writes romance novels under the penname Noelle Adams (noelle-adams.com). If you would like to contact Claire, please check out her website (clairekent.com) or email her at clairekent.writer@yahoo.com.

Books by Claire Kent

Revenge Saga
> Sweet the Sin
> Darker the Release

Escorted Series
> Escorted
> Breaking

Nameless Series
> Nameless
> Christening
> Incarnate

Hold Series
> Hold
> Release

Printed in Great Britain
by Amazon